Also by Jim Lehrer

BOOKS

Blue Hearts

A Bus of My Own

Short List

Lost and Found

The Sooner Spy

Crown Oklahoma

Kick the Can

We Were Dreamers

Viva Max!

PLAYS

The Will and Bart Show

Church Key Charlie Blue

Chili Queen

FINE LINES

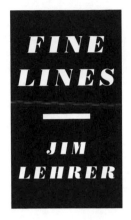

FINE
LINES

———

JIM
LEHRER

Random House
New York

Library of Congress Cataloging-in-Publication Data
Lehrer, James.
Fine lines : a novel / Jim Lehrer.
p.   cm.
ISBN 0-679-42823-2
1. One-eyed Mack (Fictitious character)—Fiction.
I. Title.
PS3562.E4419F56   1994   813'.54—dc20   93-36848

Manufactured in the United States of America
Designed by J. K. Lambert
9 8 7 6 5 4 3 2
First Edition

TO A. C. GREENE

6/13/94 Bro B.E.

FINE LINES

Chapter 1

The whole idea of an award named after a chocolate fork, no matter how coveted and prestigious, seemed a bit strange to me. But once it was explained and I read some of the material about it I began to feel proud.

I felt strongly that Jackie should not only accept the award but I should go with her to Chicago for the ceremony and the other gala events that were part of it all.

"I still wish it weren't a fork," said Jackie after we settled in on the flight to Chicago.

"Better than a hammer or a saw," I said.

"A bowl or a plate would be better."

"A fork does seem to be a rather peculiar choice."

"If it had to be a utensil I'd have preferred a spoon or a knife," she said. "They have a better feel and ring to them."

"But they'd still be chocolate," I said.

"So?"

So, congratulations.

"You're not making fun of this, are you, Mack?"

"No, ma'am. No, no, ma'am."

Jackie, my wife, was one of America's most successful women entrepreneurs. Right up there with Mary Kay, Betty Crocker and Wendy in terms of accomplishment and notoriety. She was the founding genius and chief executive officer of JackieMarts, the country's first and best drive-through grocery and convenience store. From one little place on South Western Street in Oklahoma City she had in 12 years built her franchise company into an empire of 4,347 stores in 31 states.

The Chocolate Fork was only the latest—and biggest, of course—recognition she had received for her accomplishments.

We flew to Chicago first class on American Airlines, courtesy of the Chocolate Fork for Excellence Foundation. Jackie, normally as cool about most things as she was gorgeous, was truly excited about getting a Chocolate Fork. Almost little-girl excited.

"Look at this, Mack," she said. "Can you believe it?"

In many ways Jackie, who was close to fifty (she would kill me for saying how close), still had a little-girl look and manner to her. Her short brown hair was still brown, her blues eyes still watered and shone, her slim-stacked figure could still turn heads in a crowded shopping mall.

What she was handing me there on the airplane was the program of events for the Chocolate Fork Award weekend. I had already looked at it with appreciation and wonder many times in the last few weeks. But I did so again. It told the story of how Robert Lewis Hammond III, the latest in his family to own Hammond's, the most famous chocolate company in the world, had started this award seventeen years ago to honor excellence in the individual achievement of Americans. There were small photos and biographies of Jackie and her twenty-nine fellow/sister awardees of this year. They came from all walks of life and achievement. Former President Gerald Ford. Home-run king Hank Aaron. Consumer nut Ralph Nader. Trucking magnate Hugh Newell Jacobsen. Former Secretary of State Henry Kissinger. Comedian R. Rosen. Movie star Robert Redford. Opera soprano Mary Ellen Greenfield. Race-car driver A. J. Foyt. Writer Eudora Welty. Singer Ella Fitzgerald. Dancer Gene Kelly. Plus an educational TV reporter named MacNeil, a Catholic archbishop from Milwaukee, an office-building architect, a Nobel Prize–winning physicist, a blue-jean manufacturer, a Philadelphia condominium developer and a portrait photographer I had never heard of.

Jackie was in great company with them. I was in great company with her.

The program of events said the two days of the Chocolate Fork would include a dinner Friday night—tonight—at an art museum that had a special show by some artist who did something called Urban Realism; informal dialogues all day Saturday between Jackie and the other awardees and a group of 450 hand-picked high school juniors from all fifty states, and then the final gala dinner at which the Chocolate Forks themselves would be presented.

A smiling young woman of eighteen or nineteen met us at the arrival gate at the Chicago airport, which was called O'Hare.

She wore a black skirt and a white blouse with a large brown badge in the shape of a fork over the left breast pocket. She was holding a small cardboard sign with Jackie's name on it.

"I'm Tina," she said after we identified ourselves to her. "On behalf of the Chocolate Fork, hello."

"Hello, Tina," Jackie said.

"Hello, Tina," I said.

We followed her down a wide concourse that was filled with a mass of people going to and from airplanes. I had never seen so many people going to and from airplanes. I had never seen a concourse that long. It went on and on and on. And on. Like maybe we were going to walk all the way into downtown Chicago. I was delighted that we had checked our two large suitcases, one with Jackie's dresses, the other with my things, which included a tuxedo for the gala. All we were carrying were a couple of briefcase-sized things. But even they got heavy after a while.

Arriving finally at Baggage Claim Carousel D on the lower concourse was close to arriving at the end of a hike across the panhandle of Oklahoma. I made a joke to that effect to Tina.

"There's no other way to go unless you're handicapped or old," Tina replied, glancing at the black patch over my left eye.

"Well, we're certainly not either one of those," Jackie said.

At that moment another young woman who looked and dressed like Tina came rushing up.

She had what she called a "supremely urgent important" message for the lieutenant governor of Oklahoma. That was me. The message was simply, "Call C."

I found a pay phone and called Oklahoma City for C. Harry Hayes, my friend who was the director of the Oklahoma Bureau of Investigation, the OBI.

"Somebody croaked The Cluck," C. said.

"The Cluck" was C.'s and most everyone else's nickname for State Representative Jonah Morgan, Democrat of Utoka. There was no dumber cluck member of our legislature, no dumber cluck member of any legislature, I suspected.

"Croaked?" I said.

"Shot him right between his two clucky eyes," said C. "A very neat job. The only blood was in the back . . ."

"Who did it?"

"I have no idea. We just found the body in a lobbyist's condo an hour ago. It's still more or less warm—room temperature, you might say."

"Why are you calling me? I am about to help my wife receive a Chocolate Fork."

"The Chip said to call you. I called you. Maybe he wants you to know you'll have a funeral to go to when you get back." I always had funerals to go to. It was part of my job as lieutenant governor, the Second Man of Oklahoma.

The Chip was Joe Hayman, the governor of our state, the First Man of Oklahoma. C. called Joe "The Chip," as in buffalo chip, which is what our farmers and ranchers call dried buffalo dung. It came from his real nickname, "Buffalo Joe," which came from the fact that he was from the town of Buffalo out in the Oklahoma panhandle. There were some people in the state who also said he resembled a buffalo in his physical appearance.

Joe and C. detested one another. I could imagine what was going on between them over The Cluck's murder. It made me glad to be in the Chicago airport named after somebody O'Hare.

I told Jackie that C. wanted some advice on an anticrime bill. I decided not to tell her about the killing of The Cluck in order not to ruin her big occasion.

■

Tina got us a porter and we then followed him to a long black Cadillac limousine waiting for us in a covered driveway outside. It was some limousine. It had a TV, a bar, a selection of magazines and newspapers, reading lights and a system for individually controlling the temperature of the air that blew out of little vents onto each passenger.

Just as we were about to pull away Tina appeared at the limo door.

"We have a Young Chocolate Forker who just arrived," she said. "We take them to the hotel in buses but, well, he's late. Could he ride with you? His name is David."

"Certainly," Jackie and I said almost in unison. *Certainly* was a favorite word of both of us.

David climbed in the back with Jackie and me and sat down on a jump seat facing us. He was wearing jeans and a brown checked sport coat. He had scared brown eyes, short brown hair and a terrific smile.

We introduced ourselves.

"Congratulations on winning the award," he said to me.

"My wife is the winner, not me. I'm just a lieutenant governor."

"And you, ma'am, are a governor?"

"No, no," Jackie said. "I'm a simple businesswoman."

He wanted to know about it. So she explained how a JackieMart works. How, like at McDonald's or most other fast-food restaurants, you drive up to a speaker and give your order for bread, milk and other basic convenience-store items and then drive to a window and pick it up.

"We don't have those," he said. "We still have to get out of our cars."

"Where are you from?" I asked.

"New Hampshire," David replied.

"How did you happen to become a Young Chocolate Forker?" Jackie asked.

The limo, driven by a middle-aged white man in a black uniform, was now moving out of the airport toward a freeway and downtown.

"I made a speech about democracy."

"What did you say about it?" I asked.

"The usual stuff," David replied.

Democracy. The usual stuff.

It had been only two weeks before that I had run into The

Cluck, the late Jonah Morgan of Utoka, in the state capitol building parking lot, where we lieutenant governors and legislators had reserved parking.

"Hey, hey, if it isn't the One-eyed Mack, the one-eyed hero of Oklahoma liberal utopism!" he had yelled at me. He came up to me from nowhere, from somewhere. Maybe he had been behind a tree. Or in a groundhog hole.

"Hey, Jonah," I said and stuck out my right hand.

Jonah was a man of fifty who wore the clothes of a man of fourteen. In size as well as style. Everything he had on, which looked cheap and old, was too small and too loud. He wore his dark blond hair in a crew cut. Overall, it made him look like what he was: a dumb cluck.

"I have been waiting for you to call me and thank me," he said. "It's not often we are on the same side, Oklahoma's side, America's side. But here I am and there you are and here we are."

"Thank you, Jonah," I said. "Did somebody buy you off?"

It just came out of my mouth because it had been on my mind. The Cluck had suddenly reversed his position and come out in favor of Sooner Number One, a progressive piece of legislation that would improve our public schools. It would put a three-cent increase on the sales tax, fifteen cents on cigarettes and a dollar on a case of beer to double the pay of all public school teachers in the state, pay the tuition of any teacher who took advanced graduate courses, upgrade all textbooks, triple the number of books in all school libraries, create a visiting master teacher's program in math, English and history, and set up a college scholarship program for every high school senior who scores at least 850 on his SAT, among many other things, most of which Jess had already proved successful in his town of Diamond Grove.

The Cluck let go of my hand and slapped me hard on the left shoulder. Really hard.

"If you weren't a one-eyed cripple I would pummel your torso for asking such a question," said The Cluck. "I really would. You're a pissant, Mack. A left-leaning, egg-sucking, ass-scratching, mummy-loving pissant. You know what a pissant is, Mack? Well, you ever noticed those little black things that crawl around in urinals in public rest rooms at the fairgrounds and at Texacos and Conocos? Have you ever noticed them, Mack? Well, the next time you do, think of me. Think of me as the man who said that's what you are."

"How much did Jess Deaton pay you out of his little suitcase?" Again, it just came out.

Right before my very eyes, Jonah Morgan's face turned from manila-envelope vanilla to strawberry–ice cream pink.

"I have never and I would never take so much as the dirt from the downside of a one-cent penny from that crazy communist old coot of a___!"

Democracy. The usual stuff.

■

We were taken to a massive hotel called the Morris Plaza. I wondered why so many hotels, even in Oklahoma, have plaza in their names but nowhere else in sight.

There were two written messages waiting for me at the front desk. One was to call "Mr. Hayes—Urgent," but the time on it was before our plane arrived so it was moot. The other was to call "Tommy Walt—Business."

Tommy Walt was our son. He, like his mother, was a successful entrepreneur. He had started T.W. Collections, a restaurant-grease–collection business, six years before. He, again like his mother, started small. From one part-time employee and one pickup truck in Oklahoma City, he had grown to 54 trucks and 102 employees with operations in 7 states.

"Dad, can you come to my shop Sunday afternoon, when you get back?" he said.

"For what?"

"For the most exciting demonstration of the post-oil world."

"What post-oil world?"

"The one that's coming."

"What in the world are you talking about?" I said.

"Just come, please. I need you."

"For what?"

"You'll see."

So I told him I would be there. He was my son, after all.

"They're saying on the radio that Jonah Morgan's murder may have been a mob hit," Tommy Walt said before hanging up.

"Who is saying that?"

"I don't know. On the radio news they never really say who is saying anything."

A mob hit? What self-respecting mobster would go to the trouble to kill a cluck?

■

Our hotel room was one of those luxury ones. It had white terry-cloth robes, shoe-shine mitts, memo pads and ballpoint pens, a sewing kit, baskets of shampoos and lotions, a TV set and a telephone in the bathroom, among so many other wonderful things. The only other time in my life I had stayed in such a room was when I was in New York for a Democratic convention. What this room had that the one in New York did not have was a prayer on our pillows. A most unusual prayer. It was printed on a cream-colored card in brown script-type type.

It said:

TO OUR GUESTS

In ancient times there was a prayer for "The Stranger within our gates." Because this hotel is an institution designed to serve

*people, and not solely a money making institution, we hope that
God will grant you peace and rest while you are under our roof.*

*May this room and hotel be your "second" home. May those
you love be near you in thoughts and dreams. Even though we
may not get to know you, we hope that you will be comfortable
and happy as if you were in your own house.*

*May the business that brought you our way prosper. May
every call you make and every message you receive add to your
joy. When you leave, may your journey be safe.*

*We are all travelers. From "birth till death" we travel between
the eternities. May these days be pleasant for you, profitable for
society, helpful for those you meet, and a joy to those who know
and love you best.*

I had just finished reading it aloud to Jackie, who laughed
all the way through, when the phone rang. It was C.

"Two down," he said.

"Two what?"

"Two members of the Oklahoma legislature."

The body of State Representative Willard (Tipp) Freeman,
Democrat of Ponca City, had just turned up splattered facedown on the pavement in front of the Park Plaza Hotel in
downtown Oklahoma City. It had fallen fourteen floors from a
penthouse suite on the top floor.

"We don't know if he jumped or was pushed," C. said. "The
Chip is screaming at me and everybody about God having
decided to punish the legislature for having turned down Oper-

ation Cash For Trash. The idiot." Operation Cash For Trash was Joe's proposal for selling off huge areas of barren western Oklahoma land to the Japanese for huge amounts of money for use as huge landfills for burying garbage and other waste.

I did not respond to C.'s attacks on Joe. I made it a practice never to respond to anybody's attacks on Joe.

"He said to tell you your people need you, Mack."

"My wife needs me here. Tell him I'll be home Sunday."

"Oh, yeah, the Vanilla Almond Knife or whatever it is. How's that going?"

"It's a fork. A Chocolate Fork."

"Bring me home a bite, okay, Mack?"

"Good-bye, C."

I decided not to tell Jackie about the second death of a member of our legislature in a matter of a few hours because I did not want to ruin her big event.

■

The Urban Realism artist's name was Richard Estes, as in Billy Sol Estes, the Texas fertilizer swindler of the 1960s. More than seven hundred of us awardees, spouses, Young Chocolate Forkers and guests drank and nibbled during a cocktail hour and then sat down at round tables of ten each for dinner among thirty or so of Estes's paintings. They were more like huge color photographs than paintings. I had never seen anything like them. There was one of four shiny silver telephone booths with a person in each talking on the phone. It was called "Telephone Booth." All of them were called what they were. "The Candy Store," for instance, was the window of a candy store. The fudge and the peanut brittle and the Swiss chocolate bars and the twirl lollipops were so realistic, they looked edible. Like you could reach into the painting and pull something out and stick it in your mouth. They were all that real. Somebody said they were all scenes from New York City. There were shots through the windows of diners and luncheonettes, down escalators, along streets of dry cleaners and flower shops, hardware and liquor stores.

My favorite was titled "Bus Window." It was the front of a city bus, and you could see not only the driver behind the wheel inside the bus but also the reflection in the windshield of buildings and things outside it. I had always been partial to buses, particularly the kind that went from city to city, such as Trailways, Greyhound, Jefferson and Oklahoma Blue Arrow. I had even worked in a bus depot in Adabel, Oklahoma, when I was a kid. So had Tommy Walt in Oklahoma City.

Somebody said each of Richard Estes's paintings was worth at least $150,000, which was a stunner since they really did seem more like blown-up photographs than art. But I was delighted to know that people considered pictures of real things like buses art. Except for a few pointers I picked up going to museum show openings of French or cowboy art in Oklahoma

City since I became lieutenant governor, I knew nothing at all about art. Somebody else there at the Chicago dinner said that in New York and Dallas people were paying millions for huge sculptures of things like old baseball gloves and rubber erasers and paintings of Campbell soup cans and movie stars like Marilyn Monroe. Now, that really did seem like a bit much.

Jackie's dialogue with the Young Chocolate Forkers the next morning was terrific. She followed Hank Aaron and Ralph Nader, and R. Rosen and Ella Fitzgerald followed her. Jackie told the story of how she happened to start JackieMarts—how she just one day realized how inconvenient it was to have to get out of the car to buy a loaf of bread, a carton of milk or whatever, so she decided to do something about it.

"Do the men discriminate against women businessmen in Oklahoma?" a female Young Chocolate Forker from Loudonville, Ohio, asked. Some people laughed at what she said— "women businessmen"—but I couldn't tell if she understood what they were laughing at. I hoped she couldn't.

"They're afraid to," Jackie answered, "because they know we're smarter and tougher than they are and we might decide to compete against them, and everybody knows what that would mean: bankruptcy and ruin for every businessman in Oklahoma."

That brought down the house.

A boy in a white T-shirt that said "YMCA San Antonio" on it in red asked: "Is it wrong to want to become rich?"

Jackie responded: "Yes. Because it will not work. Look at

the rich people. They got that way because they inherited it or by working hard at something they enjoyed or because they had a great idea. Some of the poorest people I know are people who decided only that they wanted to be rich. They had no other drive, no other purpose. They failed. They deserved to fail. Don't cry for them and don't do it yourself."

It made everybody understand why Jackie had been successful and why she certainly deserved a Chocolate Fork Award. I could feel it in the room, which was a huge hotel ballroom set up with a stage at one end and rows of long thin tables and chairs. To ask their questions, the kids went to microphones set up in the aisles.

R. Rosen came after Jackie. He said he became a comedian because as a kid growing up in Indianapolis, Indiana, his family's telephone number was only one digit different than that of some fancy steak house. People called them by mistake a lot and he and his brother started taking reservations with John Wayne cowboy accents. I had heard him tell it once before on the old *Jack Paar Show*. I didn't think it was funny then and I still didn't. All it made me do was feel sorry for the fine people of Indianapolis, Indiana, who showed up at the restaurant expecting to have a fine evening celebrating their wedding anniversary, birthday, promotion or whatever and were told they had no reservation.

But in all fairness to Rosen, even Bob Hope, Jack Benny and Red Skelton, together or one after another, would have had trouble making me laugh right then. Tipp Freeman was not one of my favorite members of the legislature, despite his willingness to support Sooner Number One. He was a typical The Best Government Is No Government type except when it came to a road, a bridge, a school or a project of any kind he wanted for his own district. Otherwise, if he had had his way, the capitol building would have been sold off to Kmart or Sears, our highway and law enforcement turned over to the Burns or Wackenhunt detective agencies, our schools to the Southern Baptists. I didn't care for his ambition either. He was only in his late twenties, but he was already encouraging talk about his being a governor or United States senator someday.

The important thing about him now was that he was dead. The second member of the Oklahoma legislature to die a violent, untimely death within a few hours.

Buffalo Joe delivered the news to me about the third.

■

Somebody got me out of the cocktail-party reception before the final gala dinner to take the call from Joe.

"Now there are three! One, two, three, Mack! Did you hear me? Three! A third one died! Dead! Gone! Dead! Killed! Three, Mack! One and then two and now three!"

Joe identified number three as State Representative Doug Little, Democrat of Pauls Valley. He went to his maker in the front seat of his red Pontiac Grand Am. The car went out of control on I-35 south of Norman and hit an overpass abutment at an estimated speed of eighty-five miles an hour.

"Somebody did it, Mack," Joe said. "Somebody did it."

He was speaking relatively calmly now, but I knew it wasn't going to last. I knew it was only a matter of a few more seconds before it all started again boiling over and out.

"Did what, Joe?" I asked.

"Killed him! Killed him! Fooled with the steering! Killed him! Killed him dead!"

I heard him take a breath.

"I want the killer or killers found, arrested, charged, indicted, tried, tarred, feathered, French fried, panfried, barbecued, publicly hanged, gassed and shot by firing squad," Joe said. He was now at full blast, up there where he spoke as if addressing all of Oklahoma at the same time, when he was really only talking to one person across the room or on the phone, as he was now.

"I will announce that I have asked you, the Second Man of Oklahoma, to personally oversee the investigation on my behalf, to coordinate the efforts of the OBI, the highway patrol, the FBI, the CIA, the IRS, Interpol, the sanitation departments of Tulsa, Ardmore, Weatherford and Lawton and all others you may choose to involve. On my behalf. On behalf of our people who are depending on you and me and all of the rest of the government of their state to get to the bottom of what is going on. What is going on, Mack?"

"I have no idea, Joe," I said. "I am in Chicago."

"Is there a vendetta at work against the government of our state?"

"I don't know, Joe. I am in Chicago."

He continued:

"I want it to be safe again for the servants of the people of this state to walk the streets and byways of this state, Mack. I want this wanton slaughter stopped and I want it stopped now. Murder has no place in our government."

"I hear you, Joe."

"Hearing me isn't enough, Mack. Do you know your Oklahoma history, Mack? Well, I do and I can tell you right for sure that I do. And I am telling you that this is the first time in the history of this state that three members of the Oklahoma House of Representatives have been murdered within twenty-four hours. The first time!"

"I certainly believe that."

"Believing me isn't enough, Mack. Are more coming? That is the question. That is the question, Mack. Are there more coming? Is the Senate next? And then the executive branch? You and me? You and me, Mack?"

"I am in Chicago, Joe."

"That is not the point either."

"It could be a simple coincidence of timing at work here, Joe," I said. "Maybe there was nothing that united Jonah Morgan of Utoka and Tipp Freeman of Ponca City and Doug Little of Pauls Valley except they were all three members of the Oklahoma House of Representatives."

"All were Democrats," Joe said.

"Wiping out all of the Democrats in Oklahoma, one at a time like this, would take a while, Joe," I said. "I somehow doubt if that is what we are facing here. Even Republicans are smarter than that."

"What, then? What, then?"

What, then? I'm in Chicago!

I said: "Well, Jonah could have been killed by a mad girlfriend, Tipp by a mad bill collector, Doug by a mad constituent."

"I'll bet it was a drug cartel."

"We don't have any in Oklahoma, Joe."

"What about OPEC? They're a cartel."

"They sell oil, Joe."

"I know that! Don't tell me what I already know! The mob. I heard it might be the mob."

"We don't have a real mob in Oklahoma, either."

"You're just trying to ease my fears, aren't you, Mack? That's it. Trying your best to ease my fears."

"Well, you can rest assured Hayes and the boys will get to the bottom of it in no time," I said.

"Hayes couldn't solve a kid's jigsaw puzzle of a choo-choo train," he said. "Where are you, Mack?"

"I'm in Chicago, Joe."

"Chicago! I want you here! I want you here by my side!"

"I'll be back in the morning."

"You don't carry a gun, do you, Mack? Do you carry a gun?"

"No, sir."

"Think about it, Mack. Think about carrying one. What are you going to do if you catch this killer or killers?"

"It's unlikely that I'll come across him here in Chicago."

"I know that! I told you not to tell me what I already know! What about when you get off the plane?"

"I'll think about it, Joe. I really will, although, as you know, I believe in strong gun-control laws. I believe that we need to control the sale and possession of firearms in Oklahoma and the whole country. I believe it would cut down on crime and on accidental deaths. So it would be inconsistent for me to go out and buy a gun and put it on my hip like Matt Dillon. Hey, look there, podner, if it isn't the One-eyed Mack."

"Don't raise heavy philosophy issues at a time like this," he said. "This is a government crisis, not a philosophy crisis. Can you believe the first time in history three members of the Oklahoma House of Representatives are murdered within twenty-four hours happens during our administration? The Hayman-Mack administration. The best administration in the history of Oklahoma. Can you believe that, Mack?"

I could believe that. What I could not believe was his reference to the Hayman-Mack administration. It was the first time he had done that.

Then he hit me with another law-enforcement problem that I had hoped to avoid by my absence from the state. It was one of those stupid things that I had hoped might go away on its stupid own. It had not done so.

"Get back here and stop that crazy man in Davidson, too, Mack," he said. "If he dies on us it would be another huge embarrassment to us and our state. An embarrassment is what it would be. Make sure he doesn't die. Okay, Mack? He'll listen to you. Everybody listens to you. Particularly the crazies. Particularly the crazies. They think you are really something."

"Okay, Joe."

"And those stupid mummies, Mack. People are calling and writing about those stupid mummies. . . ."

"Got to run, Joe. The big gala dinner's about to start. Got to run."

I hung up and returned to the festivities in the hotel ballroom.

That crazy man in Davidson was Digger Don Donnelly, the city marshal. He had gone on a hunger strike to protest Senate Bill 127, which would outlaw speed traps, the major source of his and his town's income.

Never mind about the mummies. Not right now.

I decided not to tell Jackie about the third killing because I didn't want to ruin her big event.

■

After the rest of us were seated for dinner, each of the thirty awardees was announced one at a time by a radio-announcer kind of guy with a radio-announcer kind of voice. The awardees walked slowly down a red carpet to a seat at a mile-long head table while appropriate band music was played. Jackie's appropriate music was "Surrey with the Fringe on Top" from the world-famous musical *Oklahoma!*

She, like all the others, wore a three-inch-wide red, white and blue ribbon sash across her front. Attached to the bottom end of the sash was a foot-long chocolate fork wrapped in heavy, shiny silver foil.

Dinner was what they serve at hotel banquets in Oklahoma and, I assume, everywhere else in the world. There was a salad with some kind of orange dressing, a boneless chicken breast with a mushroom-type sauce, a couple of small carrots, three or four green beans, a smidgen of boiled potatoes, cold hot rolls with butter and a raspberry parfait thing. I didn't drink any because I do not drink, but there was also white wine from a wine-making company in Lubbock, Texas.

A middle-aged woman TV talk-show host whom I had never seen on television was mistress of ceremonies after dinner. She read a tribute to each awardee, who then came forward, accepted the official Chocolate Fork Award and made some acceptance remarks that were not to exceed two minutes. The award itself was an eighteen-inch-long chocolate-colored fork made of fine porcelain that was framed inside an elaborate boxlike thing with the person's name on a brass plaque underneath.

I could see and hear extremely well because I was sitting at a table right down front with the spouses of three other awardees: Mrs. Rosen, Mrs. Aaron and Mrs. Kissinger. They seemed like nice ladies, very much at ease with being married to famous men, just as I was being married to a famous woman. Except for Mrs. Rosen, they talked mostly among themselves and to the others at our table. None had ever been to Oklahoma, and only Mrs. Rosen asked what I did for a living. So, she was the only one I was able to tell that I had an identity of my own as the lieutenant governor of Oklahoma, the Second Man of the Sooner State. She was also the only one who recognized me from my twenty-nine minutes on national television three years before when I delivered the keynote speech to the Democrats at Madison Square Garden in New York City, the one C. and some other people in the newspapers still called the Great Mummy Speech.

"How did the mummy thing work out?" Mrs. Rosen asked.

"Fine," I replied.

That was a lie. A big lie. It not only had not worked out fine, it had not yet worked out at all.

"Did you find it?" asked Mrs. Rosen.

"No, ma'am, we're still looking."

I had told everybody in Madison Square Garden and the world that a mummy of a man who claimed to have been John Wilkes Booth was missing from one of our Oklahoma museums. I asked everybody to help us find it and a lot of people did. It was not the smartest thing I had ever done. And it was not something I wanted to talk to Mrs. Rosen or anyone else about. Ever again, if possible, which it wasn't.

I changed the subject back to our spouses and their Chocolate Forks.

Jackie, I swear, got the loudest applause after her acceptance remarks. That was because, unlike the others, who all
used their two minutes of time or more, Jackie went to the
microphone and said only:

"Thank you very much."

Although she would have firmly denied it, she was simply
putting into practice one of Buffalo Joe's many rules of public
political life: Always speak shorter than expected. If they are
expecting forty-five minutes, speak for thirty. If ten, do five.
And so on. As Joe said, "Nobody remembers what anybody but
Abraham Lincoln said in a speech, and the only reason they
remember his at Gettysburg was because it was only seven
minutes long. Only seven minutes long, Mack. That's why
everybody liked it, and remembered it. It didn't have a thing to
do with what he said. It never does. Never. It's always how long
you talked, not what you said. Always, Mack. Always."

When, long after midnight, the last of the awardees had
accepted and spoken, they were led through the climax ritual
that the brochure said had marked these award ceremonies
since their founding by Robert Lewis Hammond seventeen
years ago.

"Will everyone, the awardees and guests here in the hall,
please stand," said the TV personality, a heavily made up
black woman in a tight dark blue evening dress and a dark-
blond wig.

The place got absolutely silent.

"Now, please, awardees, remove your sashes," said the
emcee.

I kept my eye on Jackie as she and the others lifted their sashes up and over their heads.

"Remove the wrapper from the chocolate fork."

The awardees carefully took the silver foil off their individual forks.

The emcee then said: "Now do what comes naturally."

Those were the magic words of the ceremony: Now Do What Comes Naturally.

Jackie lifted the chocolate fork to her mouth and took a big bite. So did the other awardees.

I joined with Mrs. Rosen, Mrs. Kissinger, Mrs. Aaron and the seven hundred or so others in the ballroom in giving an ovation of cheers and applause that lasted almost five minutes and that Jackie said afterward compared in noise and spirit to what the OU football team got in Norman at the end of a game in which they had just been victorious.

■

Jackie insisted on wearing her sash the next morning. She wore it as we checked out of the hotel, in the limo to the airport, on the plane and in the taxi from Will Rogers World Airport in Oklahoma City to the state capitol. After dropping me the taxi would take Jackie to her office at the international headquarters building of JackieMarts, Inc., farther north.

"I am so, so proud of this sash," she said when we parted in the car. "I don't think I can bear to ever take it off."

I laughed with sympathy and understanding.

"I mean it, Mack," she said without a smile.

And she really did.

But it was the least of my problems right then.

C. made me repeat several times what happened once I arrived at the capitol after saying good-bye to Jackie. The details were important.

I came up from the west parking lot entrance on the elevator and, as always, got off on the second floor, where my office was. I said hello to Jack Perkins, the state auditor, who was on his way to the elevator.

"Isn't it awful about The Cluck?" he said.

"Sure is," I said.

"About Tipp?"

"You bet."

"About Doug?"

"Right, Jack."

"The Tulsa papers said an Oklahoma capitol version of Jack the Ripper may be loose in our midst," he said. "The Capitol Ripper. How about that for a name?"

How about that?

I came across two middle-aged women in slacks, glasses and sneakers carrying cameras, capitol-building guidebooks and huge straw purses. They asked me where the ladies' room was. I told them, and as I did they recognized me and asked me to sign their maps of the capitol building. For several months after my Great Mummy Speech in New York a lot of people recognized me and talked to me like I was a celebrity of some kind. Most of that had worn off now and I was back to being mostly unrecognized.

I once got into a conversation with Nita Pickens of Perkins Corner, the world's first lady of country music, who was from Perkins Corner, Oklahoma. We were on the same commencement program at her alma mater, Southeastern Oklahoma State College in Hugotown. I was the commencement speaker; she was receiving a distinguished alumnus award. She told me that day that once you have been recognized a few times, the need to always be recognized gets caught in the brain and the soul forever. She had seen it over and over again in old musicians, particularly in and around Nashville.

"I heard of one old singer who went to the same Seven-eleven store day after day for eleven years because that was where he was recognized once," she said. "Nobody ever did again and he died a broken man." I had a hunch that one day I would hear that story set to music as one of her songs. Most of them were sad like that.

My conversation with Nita Pickens of Perkins Corner was before my Madison Square Garden speech, but I told her that I did not think that could ever happen to me and it hadn't.

That may have been mainly because I wasn't recognized by that many people for that long.

At the front door of my office I ran into a young woman who worked for the clerk of the House. Hi, I said, isn't it awful? Hello and yes, Mr. Lieutenant Governor, she said, making her one of only a few people who did not call me Mack, particularly after New York. Even there in the capitol building. I did not mind. Mack was who I was. It was a name I gave myself, actually, when I left Kansas when I was nineteen. "The One-eyed Mack" was the full name I made up. Mack came from the truck. In fact, in my younger years I loved to tell people that. I'm Mack, *M-a-c-k*, as in truck.

Janice Alice Montgomery, my wonderful elderly secretary, also said something about how awful the murders were and then told me Representative Johnny Whistle of Enid had already arrived and was waiting for me inside my private office. It was then—and only then—that I remembered even making the appointment with Johnny before leaving for Chicago. I told her I had to go by and see Tommy Walt, and I asked her to see if she could get Digger Donnelly on the telephone after I talked to Johnny Whistle.

Janice Alice said the governor had called and was desperate to see me. And, as usual these days, there were a couple of phone messages about the mummies. That was what Johnny Whistle had said he wanted to see me about, and that was probably why I had pretty much put the appointment out of my mind. He wanted to push me further into helping find some money for the mummies. Sandra Faye Parsons, who had gotten me into the mummies situation in the first place, had sicced him on me.

Janice Alice handed me a letter, still in a white envelope marked "Personal," that I could tell from the postmark, Enid, and the handwriting was, in fact, from Sandra Faye. Not now, Sandra Faye. Not now.

I stuck the envelope in my inside suit coat pocket and thanked Janice Alice for doing her job so well, as I always did, and went straight on back.

Johnny Whistle of Enid was sitting in a chair with his back to the door.

"Hi, Johnny," I said and headed toward my desk.

Johnny made no sound, no movement. He was slouching forward.

Then I noticed the ribbon. A two-inch-wide red ribbon with "Boomer Sooner" written across it in white. It was tied tightly around Johnny Whistle's neck.

His face was a dull bluish-white. His gray eyes were goo-gah wide-open as if he simply could not believe what had just happened to him.

Which was that somebody had strangled him to death with that red and white ribbon.

■

I am not going to repeat here everything the governor said when I told him about Johnny Whistle. Joe Hayman was not a man who used a lot of profanity, so what he said was even more stunning than it might have been otherwise. It's enough to say that it was the most unusual mixture of sexual and animal and scatological words, phrases and noises I had ever heard.

He also threw a few things against the walls in his office, the heaviest being a silver-framed photo of his wife, a heavy woman with a singing voice comparable to Kate Smith's. Or so they said. I personally never thought she was that good, but it was not for me to say. I was not a music critic.

"The ___ Capitol Ripper ___ killer is running and ___ loose in this sacred ___ building, Mack! The ___ Capitol ___ Ripper killer of legislators is right here in the ___ state capitol building! Right here under our ___ noses and ___!

"This is it, Mack! ___! I mean it—*i-t*-it! No more! No more!"

I knew he meant murders. No more murders.

"Stop it, Mack! Stop it!"

"I will, Joe. I will."

"___! If you hadn't been off in Kansas City eating and ___ dog ___-flavored spoons and ___ pigs and cats and things this would never have happened!"

"I was in Chicago, Joe. They were forks. Chocolate forks. Jackie received one."

"You let me down, Mack! You ___ me and my office! You let the people of the Sooner State down! You got them down and you ___ to their ___ and you ___ their ___! If you had been here this would never have happened! ___, Mack! I told you you were in charge! I told you to stop it! But you stayed away, Mack! You stayed up there in Milwaukee sipping and ___ on horse ___–flavored can openers and sticking them up every ___ and ___ and or whatevers!"

Then suddenly he stopped yelling and throwing things. The coloring in his face returned to its normal pale white from its temporary state of red. I immediately recognized what had happened. He had just had an idea.

In a quiet voice, almost a whisper, he said:

"I am not here, Mack. I am at the bedside of my dying mother in Buffalo. I was called away in the middle of the night. I will return this afternoon after your call about the untimely murder of Johnny Whistle of Enid. It was untimely, Mack. Very untimely for the Hayman-Mack administration. But you are in charge of this matter. You, our beloved lieutenant governor. You, the man who put mummies on the map of Oklahoma and of the United States of America, are in charge. If you can't do it, Mack, nobody can. If you can't do it, Mack, nobody can."

He walked to the window and looked beyond Petunia #1, the only pumping oil well on the grounds of any state capitol, toward the skyline of downtown Oklahoma City twenty blocks away.

"Did you ever dream anything this awful would ever happen? A crime wave to end all crime waves. A crime wave against elected officials of the great Sooner State of Oklahoma. How could we have known it would happen? It's not our fault, Mack. We must tell the people it's not our fault. We must tell them we might even be in danger. We, the governor and the lieutenant governor, the First and Second Men of their state, the people who pave their roads and fry their convicts, could be in danger, too. There's a madman out there. A madman who hates the dedicated public servants of this state, the people who steal from the poor and give it to the rich—or whatever. A madman, Mack. A madman. And maybe there's more than one. Think about that, Mack. A whole army of madmen out there, probably slipped over the border from Arkansas or Texas, to wipe out our duly elected and honestly sworn government of Oklahoma."

He turned back to me.

"I will be in my office at the capitol by late this afternoon, Mr. Lieutenant Governor. I will be expecting a full report on the progress of the investigation."

"You are in your office right now, Joe. Aren't there people who know you're here . . ."

"Shut up, Mack! And get the ___ ___ ___ out of here!"

Jackie, C. and others had been increasingly persistent in recent months in insisting that Joe was losing his grip on his life and his office. Some people had even—joking, really— suggested I stage a little bloodless revolt. Just walk in there one morning and take over the governor's office and the government.

I had steadfastly refused even to listen to such talk. But at that moment, as I walked from his office, where he said he wasn't, I was not so steadfast.

It must be said in Joe's defense, though, that the untimely killing within forty-eight hours of four members of the legislature, one by ribbon strangulation while he sat in the middle of the office of the lieutenant governor, might have been enough to drive anybody crazy.

There was a small mob in front of my office door, which was glass with the state seal of Oklahoma and my name painted on it. The mob consisted of about twenty-five capitol and OCPD officers in uniform, reporters, TV and newspaper photographers, officials, clerks and secretaries from offices all over the capitol.

The reporters yelled questions at me and the photographers turned on their bright lights to take pictures of me. I looked grim, said nothing and pushed my way through them and back inside.

C. and scads of other men in frowns and suits were there in the outer office. C. was delighted to see me. He wanted to hear my story, so he and Jack Severn of OCPD took me into my private office to the scene of the crime. Johnny Whistle of Enid was still dead in the chair. People in police uniforms and plain-clothes scurried around taking pictures, picking up things with tweezers, putting things in envelopes.

I told C. and Jack exactly what happened from the time I parked my car in the west lot.

"What was he doing in here by himself?" Detective Severn asked.

I told him about the appointment to talk about various things, which I had forgotten about, really. I said nothing about the mummies. I tried never to say anything about the mummies.

We walked over to a door that opened onto the stairwell that went from the first to the second floor there on the south side of the capitol. It was an unmarked entrance and exit that I sometimes used to avoid people waiting for me in the outer office. Most everyone knew about the thing, so it was hardly any kind of secret passage.

C. opened it, but not wide enough to see much on the other side. I could tell there were people out there on the wide old marble steps, but I could not really see them. The murder of a fourth member of the Oklahoma legislature in forty-eight hours had drawn a crowd.

"Janice Alice told me she opened the office herself this morning and never left," C. said. "She said nobody but Whistle came in through the front, so that means the killer or killers came and went through this door."

"Who knew about the door?" Severn asked.

"Everybody," I replied.

"Was it locked?"

"At night," I said, "but one of the first things Janice Alice does in the morning is unlock it in case I want to use it."

"She said she unlocked it this morning per usual," C. said.

At that moment a young man in a crew cut and suit whom I recognized as an OBI agent came up to me and said that my wife was on the phone. He said she was in an excited state and was demanding to talk to me. "She said she'd come over here and pull off one of my ears so I could be like my boss if I didn't get you," said the agent.

Jackie and C. kidded around between them a lot.

"Tell Jackie that one-eared remarks are offensive to me," C. said to me. "Tell her it's a slur and if she doesn't stop it I will rally the one-eared people of Oklahoma to picket JackieMarts all over this state."

I took the call back out in the outer office. I was not about to have a phone conversation at my desk looking over at Johnny Whistle of Enid with a red and white ribbon around his neck.

Jackie's voice was high-pitched, frantic. "There's been a murder in your office?"

"Yes, but it's over."

"Over? There was a murder and it is over? Over? Are you okay?"

"Yes, I'm fine. Just fine," I said. "Johnny Whistle of Enid was killed."

"In your office? Somebody came running in here a while ago screaming he heard on a radio back in the warehouse that there had been a murder in the lieutenant governor's office. I told her nothing ever happens in the lieutenant governor's office. . . ."

"I'm fine."

"Somebody came in your office and started shooting a gun?" she asked.

"No, no, it was nothing like that. Johnny was strangled."

"Strangled? Oh, Mack, how?"

"With a red and white sash."

I said it without thinking. It just came out.

"That's not funny, Mack. How can you joke at a time like this?"

"I'm serious."

I heard only breathing for a second or two.

"You are telling me that Johnny Whistle of Enid was strangled to death in your office by somebody using a sash?"

"A wide OU ribbon, red and white. Like a sash. It was wrapped around his neck by a person or persons unknown."

Some more breathing.

"Well, I'm glad it was Johnny Whistle instead of you."

"Thank you."

I told her about Joe's holding me even more responsible for the investigation of all four killings.

"Four?" she screamed. "Four people were strangled to death in your office with OU ribbons?"

No, I said. It had completely skipped my mind that I had not told her about the first three deaths. So I now told her about The Cluck, Tipp Freeman and Doug Little and how they died.

"Why didn't you tell me about them?" Her voice was more than frantic. I am sure I could have heard her loud and clear without the telephone even though her office was twenty blocks away.

"I didn't want to ruin your big event."

She yelled and we talked a few more seconds before getting ready to say our good-byes.

"What's going on, Mack?" she asked finally.

"Like I told Joe . . ."

"Don't tell me what you told that idiot!"

"All right, all right. What's going on is a mad conspiracy among a person or persons unknown to destroy the government of our state. They have started with the Democrats in the House of Representatives. Next will come the Republicans and then the Senate. Then the Oklahoma Supreme Court, the heads of various state agencies. I figure they'll get to me in about four months—on the second Tuesday in October." I stopped talking for a couple of seconds and then said: "I do not know what's going on, Jackie."

"I think being around Joe is having an effect on you, Mack. I really do. I am serious. You are sounding extremely peculiar. Never ever say anything to me about wearing a sash in public. Never do it again, Mack."

"Having walked in and found a member of the legislature sitting in your office with a red and white ribbon tied around his dead neck would make anybody sound peculiar, don't you think?"

"Good point."

We agreed to talk more over dinner and set a time to meet at Somewhere Over the Rainbow.

I hung up the phone just in time to watch Johnny Whistle of Enid leave the scene of his murder. He was riding on top of an ambulance stretcher on wheels covered with a green cloth sheet.

In a few seconds C. was by my side. With his eyes he motioned me to follow him. I did, to a far corner of the outer office behind a row of dark green metal filing cases.

"Something peculiar has turned up on The Cluck," he said in a quiet voice. "That town house where he died. He had told everybody he was borrowing it from a barber and beauticians' lobbyist."

"So?"

"He lied. No lobbyist, for the barbers and the beauticians or any other kind, has been close to it. Somebody named Cushing rented it. The rental agent said a well-dressed man in his mid-thirties came in two weeks ago and paid the deposit and two months' rent in cash. The only Cushing we've been able to find is that town between Stillwater and Tulsa. And towns don't rent town houses."

"You're right, C."

He didn't know what I meant. "I'm right about what?" he said.

"About it being peculiar."

Everything in my life at that moment seemed peculiar.

C. and Severn decided it was time for a Show, Tell and Pray session on the murders. They agreed on four o'clock.

"Since The Chip has put you in charge, Mack, you are more than welcome to join us," C. said.

I told them I would be there.

■

"Digger Donnelly's office is on line two!" Janice Alice yelled at me. I normally dialed my own calls, but this time I figured it might help to have somebody say, "The lieutenant governor is calling."

There was a woman on the phone from the city hall in Davidson. It took a while to convince her I really was the lieutenant governor of her state before she put Digger Don Donnelly on the line. She referred to him as "The Marshal," like he was Matt Dillon.

And so did he.

"This is The Marshal," said a man's voice. It was the weak

voice of a sick man. "I ain't stopping nothing until you stop what is going on up there in Oklahoma City."

"This is the lieutenant governor," I said calmly, lieutenant governor-ly. "The governor asked me to see how your health was holding up."

"Tell him I am dying, Mack. Tell him people who do not eat food die. I am not eating food, so that means I am dying. Even a Democrat should be able to figure out that kind of thing. Speaking of Democrats, I hear they're dropping like flies up there in Oklahoma City of things other than hunger. May be the best thing that ever happened to the state of Oklahoma. No offense, Mack."

Very funny, Marshal Digger Don Donnelly. He was a Republican, the only declared one to hold office as a city marshal in Oklahoma even though there were several others who acted like they were Republicans. Digger and I had met once when I was in nearby Pauls Valley for a Kiwanis speech. He called me Mack not because he knew me but because, like I said earlier, that is what most everybody called me.

"The governor and I urge you to eat, Marshal. We can work this out."

"Will he promise to veto that bill if those fools in the legislature pass it?"

"Government cannot operate by threat, Marshal. Hunger strikes cannot be the way to get legislation passed or killed. That is not how democracy works in Oklahoma or anywhere else."

"Good-bye," said the voice of Digger Don Donnelly.

The sound of the dial tone came on as I wondered how he got the nickname "Digger." I decided to ask him when I saw him, which I knew was going to have to be pretty soon if it was going to be outside a casket.

All in a day's work for the Second Man of Oklahoma.

Now it was on to doing what was all in a day's work for a father of a son in the restaurant-grease–collecting business.

■

Tommy Walt introduced me to a professor and to a car. The professor taught chemical engineering at Oklahoma State in Stillwater. His name was Snyder. The car was a seven-year-old dark cream Mercedes-Benz four-door sedan.

All three were waiting for me in the parking lot in front of T.W. Collections headquarters, a one-story dark green corrugated steel building about half the size of a football field.

"You are not going to believe what the professor here has done," said Tommy Walt as he introduced me to Snyder, a bushy-haired man in his early thirties equipped with a beard, an orange jumpsuit and white sneakers. "It is incredible, Mack. It really is."

Mack was what he called me. Tommy Walt was not my natural son. He was Pepper's. Tom Bell Pepper Bowen was my best friend and Jackie's first husband who died a Marine hero in the Korean War. He died because he jumped on a hand grenade that a Red Chinaman threw in the middle of him and some other Marines. The Congressional Medal of Honor that they gave Jackie afterward was in a small black case that we kept on a bookcase shelf in our living room. Jackie was pregnant with Tommy Walt and his twin sister, Walterene, when word came of Pepper's death. For the first twenty-seven years of his life Tommy Walt called me "Dad." He switched to "Mack" one day out of the blue after my big New York City speech on grounds that it did not make sense for him to be the only person in Oklahoma who did not call me Mack. It annoyed me and even embarrassed me a bit, to be honest about it, when he did it in front of people. Like now with the professor.

I walked with the two of them over to the rear of the Mercedes-Benz, which is an expensive German car that in Oklahoma mostly only lawyers and bail bondsmen owned. There were two large ten-gallon drums of liquid there. Both were painted bright red and had "T.W. Collections" painted across them in bright white. A much smaller bucket sat on the ground between them. It was empty.

"See that," Tommy Walt said, pointing to one of the drums. "That is old restaurant grease—our bread and butter. It was collected just four hours ago from a Burger King in Edmond."

Good.

He pointed to the other drum. "In that one is methanol."

Methanol. Terrific.

"This car," said Tommy Walt, "is a diesel."

Diesel. Great.

"Now watch this," Tommy Walt said. He nodded to Professor Snyder.

The professor took a large soup-ladle thing and dipped it into the drum of Burger King grease. He ladled one, two, three, four, five, six, seven full spoons of the smelly, awful liquid into the empty bucket.

Terrific.

"Now this," said Tommy Walt.

The professor moved to the drum of methanol. One, two, three, four, five, six, seven spoonfuls of methanol were ladled into the bucket with the grease. It looked like the messes you see behind filling stations in small towns. He mixed the liquids together for a few turns.

"Now," Tommy Walt said.

Now the professor picked up the bucket and carried it to the right rear fender of the Mercedes-Benz, where the gas tank was. The lid was off and a cone-shaped siphon was sticking out of it. He lifted the bucket and poured in the mixture of methanol and Burger King grease.

"Come with me, Mack," Tommy Walt said with about as big a grin as I had ever seen on his or maybe any other face. He was very small in stature, only five feet six inches tall, so a big smile took him over. It was great.

I followed him around to the front left side of the car. He

opened the front door and swept his right arm down in front of him. "Be my guest, sir," he said.

I got in behind the wheel.

"Turn on the key and see what happens, Mack."

I turned the ignition key to the right. There was a whurr-whurr, a slight pop and then a roar. The motor was on and running.

"Do you believe it, Mack?" Tommy Walt said. "Do you believe it?"

I believed it. I could hear and feel the diesel engine of that Mercedes-Benz.

"It's a revolution!" Tommy Walt yelled. "America will never be the same! The grease-collection business will never be the same!"

He raced around to the other side of the car and slipped into the front passenger seat. Professor Snyder jumped into the back.

Tommy Walt said: "It's a miracle, Mack, and Professor Snyder here and two other professors in Colorado and another in Denmark have discovered it. You put methanol with old grease and, bingo, you've got a fuel that runs diesel engines. Bingo. Explain it, Professor."

Denmark?

Professor Snyder said: "It's a process called transesterification." The rest of what he said I could not follow and mostly made me grateful I was not a chemical-engineering major at OSU.

Then, finally, came the pitch.

"Mack, I need you," said Tommy Walt. "We need to demonstrate this in a dramatic way, a way that will catch the eye of Oklahoma, Washington and the world."

He paused, took a breath.

"What better way than by doing it with buses. A whole fleet of buses. A whole fleet of buses like, say, those of, well, the Oklahoma Blue Arrow."

Oh, my.

"And, as you know better than anyone on the face of this Oklahoma earth, I really could not make a direct approach to them."

Oh, yes, indeed, I knew that better than anyone on the face of this Oklahoma earth. Tommy Walt, as I mentioned before, had worked for a short while at the Oklahoma City bus depot, which was run by Oklahoma Blue Arrow, our state's largest and best independent bus company. He did it only because of me. I was interested in buses and in baseball, so I pushed him right out of college into working as a bus baggage agent and playing ball for The Buses, Oklahoma Blue Arrow's semipro baseball team. It was a double disaster. He hated fooling with baggage and, in fact, it drove him to throwing bags through a bus-depot window. He also hated playing baseball because he could not hit a curve or judge a high fly ball. At my urging he turned to pitching, but that didn't work either. Tommy Walt's fingers were too small to get a good grip on the ball. It takes fingers to be a pitcher.

So he went to work for JackieMart, did great and then struck out on his own into collecting old restaurant grease for recycling into soap and other useful things.

"Would you make the contact for me at Blue Arrow?" he asked.

"Oh, I am afraid too much water may have poured under that bridge. . . ."

"Please, Mack. Please."

"I can't believe they would agree to putting old Burger King grease down their gas tanks. . . ."

"Please try. Please . . . Dad."

How could I say no? He was my son, after all.

And before I left he took me aside for one private father-son–type question.

"I talked to Mom a while ago and she said she was wearing a chocolate fork sash thing around her office," he said. "Is that true?"

"I'm afraid so, Son."

"She'll be the laughingstock of the business world, Mack. You must get her to stop that."

I promised to work on that, too.

■

I had never before seen a large color photograph of somebody's face with a bullet hole between the eyes. The hole in The Cluck was about the size of a nickel. There were little specks of blood around it, but otherwise it was much more tidy than I would have expected. It looked more like somebody burned the hole in his head with a lighted cigar than shot him. There was plenty of blood all right, but it was in the back, underneath the back of his head, where the bullet had come out. His eyes were a bright blue, something I had never noticed before. Now it was impossible to miss because they were open wide and bright like two blue headlights shining out at the world from that medical examiner's photograph.

It was on the table along with several other photos and items of physical evidence that had been gathered thus far. It was four o'clock, and C. had assembled his and Jack Severn's top investigators and technicians in the conference room at OBI headquarters for what he called a Show, Tell and Pray session. Show what was known and suspected about the four murders, Tell each other the unanswered questions and Pray together for answers.

There were ten of us around a long gray table. Everything at OBI headquarters, like its director, was dressed in gray. The ten included me and Buck Sporne, a slick-haired guy in a brown suit who C. introduced to me and the others as a special agent of the Federal Bureau of Investigation in Washington.

The order of discussion was chronological, so the demise of The Cluck was first on the agenda. One of Jack's and one of C.'s men went through what was known. The bullet was fired from close range by a .32-caliber automatic while The Cluck lay on a couch. There was no sign of forced entry or a struggle. Nothing of value from the town house was missing. The FBI had not reported back on all fingerprint matches, but so far nothing unusual or helpful. A background check on The Cluck showed no personal problems with a wife or a family member or a business associate that could have prompted murder.

"Although," said the OBI agent, a man of forty in a crew cut, "we did ascertain that the deceased was not the most popular member among his peers and colleagues in the political and legislative arena."

The agent then told me something everybody else in the room apparently already knew. A small TV camera and a lot of other electronic equipment were found in an otherwise empty bedroom on the second floor of the town house.

I expressed surprise and C. said: "That camera had a perfect view through a light fixture of everything that happened down in the living room, including the couch where The Cluck got it between the eyes."

"You mean the killing was taped—recorded on tape like for the nightly news?"

"It could have been, but if it was the tape wasn't there and we haven't found it yet. Right?"

The agent confirmed that.

"What does it mean?" I asked.

"That is what we are trying to find out, Mack," C. said, turning back to his man. "Have you traced the equipment?"

"No, sir. It's sophisticated but fairly common."

"Do you have a suspect of any kind, shape or form?" C. asked.

Everybody shook their heads.

"A wild guess?" Jack Severn asked.

Everybody shook their heads.

The report on Willard (Tipp) Freeman of Ponca City was similar. Nothing much was known except that he went through a window of the Park Plaza. The two-bedroom suite had been rented by phone that morning by Freeman. He showed up an hour later with no luggage to get a key and sign the register.

There was no sign of a struggle and no evidence of forced entry. The detectives said suicide was possible, although no note had been found and no one had come forward yet with any information that would support a suicide thesis. There were also no clean prints around the window. It would have been difficult, but not impossible, for Freeman to have gotten up and out of there without touching something. He was not wearing gloves. He was single and nothing had surfaced that would indicate he even had a girlfriend, much less an angry one with a reason to kill him. Nothing else had turned up so far. No suspects.

The color photographs of him were ghastly. There were a few of him spread out there facedown on the pavement with his arms and legs off in all directions. There was blood around him like a dark red frame that had been handcrafted to fit the many curves and grooves of his body. There were some photos of his front, taken obviously after somebody had turned him over, that I did not look at. In life his face was rather soft and boyish. There was no telling what it looked like in death, and I was not interested in seeing it.

The pictures on Doug Little resembled the kind we saw every night on the local TV news. Little's car, a red Pontiac, looked like it had been stepped on and squashed by a giant foot. His body, which I only glanced at, was in pretty much the same condition. The detectives said it seemed fairly likely that the car's steering system was damaged before the crash. First inspection by experts seemed to indicate it had been done intentionally. The key words, said the detective doing the Show, were "seemed to indicate," because they did not know for sure yet how it might have been done. So, in other words, it appeared he was murdered, but an accident had not been fully ruled out. Not yet. Also, he was in severe financial trouble because of some gambling debts he had incurred from betting on the horses at Oaklawn, the racetrack in Hot Springs, Arkansas.

"Could he have damaged his own car?" C. asked.

"It's possible, sir," said the detective in charge. "It shouldn't be ruled out."

"Were any of his creditors hoods who kill their bad debt-ors?"

"Not that we know of."

Two other detectives went through the Show part on Johnny Whistle of Enid. The work had just begun. They had established the fact that the red and white OU ribbon was sold at more than thirty-five locations in the Oklahoma City area alone. All of them were being checked, but, as one of the detectives said, they weren't hopeful of finding anything unless the person who bought them told the clerk, "Look, just in case you're interested, I'm going to use this ribbon to strangle a member of the legislature named Whistle." That brought a laugh around the table, one of the few of the meeting. No prints or physical evidence had been found. No witness had turned up who saw anybody come in or out of my back office door. Whistle, too, appeared to have no personal or professional enemies who had obvious motives to do away with him. The officers had no suspects.

C. then went around the table "looking for dovetails."

Did any two of them grow up together, go to the same college together, serve in the military together, do anything together except serve in the legislature? No. What about church? No. Were they personal friends? No. Did any two of them see the same woman or women? Not that we know. Find out. Yes, sir.

Did any of the others besides Little gamble at Hot Springs? We'll find out.

Did they have the same banker? We'll find out. The same lawyer? We'll find out. Accountant? We'll find out.

With a glance at me as if I might be able to help, C. turned to the politics of the four.

"All were Democrats, right?" C. asked.

Everyone, including me, nodded.

"All very conservative?"

"Very conservative," I said, meaning they were so far to the right they were near-lunatics, in my opinion.

"Our kind of people," Jack Severn said. Most everyone around the table laughed. Most everyone but me. They were certainly not my kind of people, my kind of Democrats, although it was a fact I kept pretty much to myself and Jackie. I believed that government did have a legitimate place in the lives of Oklahomans, most particularly when it came to education. I believed guns should be controlled. I believed women should make the decision about abortions. I believed a lot of things that not many of my political colleagues believed. That was why The Cluck called me a liberal. That's what he called everybody who disagreed with him on anything. It was the worst thing you could be called in Oklahoma, but nobody seemed to mind with me. Maybe it was because it was The Cluck who called me that or because of the New York speech or just because I was only the lieutenant governor.

C. asked me about the committee assignments and a few other things about the work of the four dead men in the legislature that might dove or tail.

"You were on the other side of most everything from all four of them, Mack," C. said. "Maybe you killed them."

"I was in Chicago."

"Right, right. Picking up the coveted Pineapple Hammer Award or something."

"Fork. It was a fork. And it was chocolate, not pineapple, and Jackie received it, not me."

Hammer. Oh, yes, hammer. Hammers. That reminded me of something I should have thought of before. Hammers.

I started thinking about hammers. Lots and lots of hammers.

It was clear nothing was clear at the meeting, and C. asked everyone at the table: "So, no patterns, no doves, no tails?"

"That's what it looks like as of right now," Severn said, speaking for everyone else.

And that brought it to Pray time.

"Does anybody have a theory, an idea, an anything he would like to throw out for discussion?" C. asked.

Silence in the room.

"Come on," C. said. "Somebody must have seen or heard something that caused something to whirl around."

Silence in the room.

C. let it hang there as he moved his head and eyes up one side of the table and down the other, looking for somebody to at least say something with their eyes that he could pick up on. There was nothing. Until he got to Buck Sporne, the

FBI man. I hadn't paid much attention to him until then because he had not said a word and he sat back from the table two or three chairs down to my left out of my line of sight. Now I saw C. look at him. They locked eyes for a couple of counts, C. moved on to the next man and then, suddenly, came back to Buck. Buck, a man with a smiling tan face, did not change expression.

C. was on his feet.

"Well, clearly we have our work cut out," he said to all. "Don't let me keep you any longer from it."

It was an abrupt ending. Strangely so. In a matter of only a few minutes the room was cleared except for C. and me. Buck was the last one to leave. He said to C.: "You look like a man with something on his mind, suh." Buck Sporne of the FBI spoke with a Deep South accent. I didn't know where he was from, but it was clearly someplace east of Arkansas.

"If you know something you are not telling me, I am going to be very unhappy when I do find it out," C. said. "And rest assured, Mr. Sporne, I will find it out."

Sporne gave C. a bow of the head and left.

And I said to C.: "What was that all about?"

"Maybe nothing, maybe everything. He is not your normal run-of-the-mill Bureau man. He's from Washington, from their government integrity division. He showed up here a while ago and asked if he could sit in. Said he might be of some technical help. Most unusual."

"What's he doing here in Oklahoma?"

"That's what I want to know."

"I thought you'all and the FBI were on the same side."

"We are except when they're investigating us."

"Us?"

"Us public servants."

That made me think even harder about hammers.

HAMMERS

Chapter 3

The national distribution center and warehouse for the Diamond Grove Hammer Corporation was in a light industrial district southwest of downtown Oklahoma City near the stockyards. I had called ahead to make sure Jess Deaton was there and not back in Diamond Grove, where he usually was.

He met me at the front door.

"Ever been around a lot of hammers at one time, Mack?" he asked me.

"No," said I.

"Well, follow me."

I did as I was told through a door into the warehouse.

"There are eleven thousand hammers in this building, of all sizes, kinds and types, all being readied to be shipped to distributors and hardware stores in all of the fifty states, Mexico, Canada and thirty-two other foreign countries," he said. "Think about that, Mack."

I tried to but my imagination wasn't good enough. I could

not see eleven thousand hammers going off to hardware stores in fifty states and all of those other places. I couldn't even see eleven thousand hammers. I looked around and saw mostly only cardboard boxes and wooden crates stacked one on another in tall and neatly organized stacks.

I also noticed there was music playing. It was coming out of speakers in all corners and crevices of the building. It was classical violin music. That was one of Jess Deaton's peculiarities. He loved classical violin music and had it playing most everywhere he was if he could manage it.

Jess was dressed his typical way, which was in tan work clothes and dark brown cowboy boots. His face was more tan than either his clothes or his boots and his hair was solid white and longer than a man his age should have worn it. The only thing on him that was expensive was his belt buckle. It was a heavy pewter kind of silver in the shape of the state of Oklahoma. There was a diamond the size of a dime down where Diamond Grove was.

"Who's killing our legislators, Jess?" I said after we had taken a few slow steps into the warehouse.

He coughed.

Jess Deaton was seventy-two years old and had a back problem in addition to whatever it was that made him cough constantly into a dirty red handkerchief. He always coughed into a dirty, colored handkerchief. It was as much his trademark as the belt buckle and the suitcase of money he had been carrying when he showed up in Diamond Grove twelve years ago. He had been born and raised in Diamond Grove and then left at the age of seventeen not to be heard from until his sudden and mysterious return.

"You really ought to do something about that cough," I said, as I always did when he coughed in front of me.

And he replied, "I am. I am going to die," as he always replied.

"All four of the victims were against Sooner Number One, then they changed their minds and came out for it and then they died." I had irresponsibly chosen to mostly ignore why The Cluck and the others had suddenly come over to our side. Jess had bought them. I knew it, but I didn't say it, not even to myself until now. That made me as guilty of bribery as Jess was. It really did. I knew it.

We were still walking among the boxes of hammers.

"You bribed the four of them to change their minds, didn't you, Jess?" I said.

"I have nothing to say."

"We had a deal. We win it fair and square or we don't win it. I don't believe in bribery, and even if I did it is against the laws that I have sworn to uphold."

He coughed into his handkerchief again and said, "I have nothing to say."

"The Cluck," I said. "I cannot believe you got The Cluck. And Johnny Whistle and Tipp? You must have had to really empty out that suitcase."

"I'm not saying anything," said Jess. "You wearing a wire?"

"A wire? You mean a recorder?"

"I mean has your one-eared friend C. Harry Hayes outfitted his one-eyed friend in a tape recorder?" And he coughed.

"No."

"Are we off the record?"

"I am the lieutenant governor, Jess. I cannot and will not condone bribery or any other violations of the law. Nothing about any crime, large or small, can or will ever be off the record with me. And that includes murder, by the way. Most assuredly, that includes murder, Jess."

And the violins played on.

He smiled, put his hands together as before God and said, "No man talks like that unless he's wearing a wire."

"Shut up, Jess."

It had taken three or four years of dealing with Jess before I could talk to him that directly, which was the only way to talk to him. At first, because he was so rich, Buffalo Joe mostly handled him. But eventually, because Jess was so strange, Joe handed him off to me, saying, "The only thing that rubs off a rich crazy man is the crazy. You come into it poor and normal and leave poor and crazy."

I hadn't minded Jess Deaton's strangeness because he used his money to turn the small Oklahoma town of Diamond Grove and its schools into the finest in Oklahoma if not in all of America. He did that instead of buying helicopters, football teams, boats and women. Now, with Sooner Number One, he was trying to do the same for the whole state.

"Ask yourself just one question, Mack," he said. "Why would a somebody who had successfully bribed another somebody then turn around and murder that somebody he had just bribed? Ask yourself that one question."

I had. He was right. It did not make sense. But I was certain there was some kind of connection, a dove and a tail. That was why I was here.

Jess wandered off toward a corner of the huge warehouse where there were boxes and crates that were open. I followed him.

"Look at this," he said, picking up a regular claw hammer, the kind everybody uses to hammer ordinary nails and things. "See this handle?"

I saw the handle. It was covered in heavy red rubber.

"The whole thing is one piece of steel. Be careful when you buy a hammer with a wooden handle. If it's not good wood it'll break, fly off and do all kinds of other things that are dangerous and nonproductive. The best are these." Jess held one out for me to hold. I took it. It felt like a great hammer to me.

He showed me sledge hammers, dead-blow hammers, bronze hammers, copper hammers, soft-face hammers, tack hammers, plastic-tipped hammers, rubber-headed hammers, mining hammers, mason's hammers, jeweler's hammers, ball-peen hammers. There were huge and heavy and black hammers, and others that were tiny and light and even painted light colors like beige.

"Nobody makes a better hammer of any kind or style any-where in the world," said Jess. "You should be proud to be the lieutenant governor of a state that has a company that can make such a statement."

"I am, Jess," I replied. "Sometimes it makes me want to go out and hammer, hammer, hammer everything in sight with every kind of hammer available from Diamond Grove."

Jess looked at me with disgust. He took one of the regular steel-claw hammers and said, "Watch this."

He tossed it underhand some twenty feet away. It hit the concrete floor with a clank. "Jackson!" he yelled. "Show him."

A middle-aged man with a shaved bald head came out of nowhere in a green pickup and ran over the hammer, back and forth, nine times. Then he—I assumed he was Jackson—climbed out, picked up the hammer and tossed it back toward us. Jess picked it up and showed it to us. "Not a scratch, right?" he said.

Not a scratch, right, we nodded in amazement and awe.

Not a scratch on anything.

■

There was absolutely nothing that had happened to me in the last several hours that was funny. But suddenly, there behind the wheel of my blue Buick Skylark, I broke up. Not down, which would have made more sense, but up. It was triggered by dinner. I was on my way to meet Jackie at the Somewhere

Over the Rainbow Café and I started trying to think of the last time we had a home-cooked meal at our own home. The last time Jackie and I actually fried a potato, cracked and cooked some green beans, grilled a peanut butter sandwich, roasted a roast or anything like any of that. Anything above popping some popcorn in the microwave or heating up a corn muffin in the toaster oven. Anything. Was it three years ago in April that I threw those two pork chops in a skillet, baked two potatoes and Jackie made a mixed salad of lettuce, tomato and some green peppers with a creamy white dressing called goddess? April, right. A Tuesday night? No, it was a Thursday. Then there was the time I mashed out two hamburger patties to cook outside. But it rained, so I stuck them in the broiler. When was that? Four years ago? No way. Just two, maybe.

And I smiled. Just a little smile at first. Then a big one. I sniffed and I snapped and I jerked. And laughed. A tiny laugh at first, just to myself. It grew to a hearty, healthy one, then to a guffaw and finally to giggles and tears. Giggles and tears that I could not turn off.

It was crazy. Jess, Joe, Tommy Walt, sashes, hammers and four killings by a person or persons unknown were making me as crazy as everyone else.

The Somewhere Over the Rainbow Café was one of our many favorite places to eat. It was a fancy hamburger place devoted to the memory and the music and the spirit of the one, the only, Judy Garland. She had no connection to Oklahoma City or to Oklahoma, but she did to an old theater man who claimed he had once traveled with Judy on one of her cross-country singing tours. He also winked and hinted that there had been more to the relationship than simply traveling and business. Nobody I knew believed any of that, but nobody cared either. The important thing was that he played her music in the restaurant all the time. The walls were plastered with movie posters and photographs of Judy as a girl, as a young singer, as an aging actress. The menu was seventeen different hamburgers, each named for something having to do with Judy. A Star Is Born Burger, for instance, was raw hamburger meat between two pieces of French bread. A You Made Me Love You Burger had three well-done patties layered among four pieces of sesame bun, four kinds of sliced cheese, lettuce, tomato, onion, mustard, olives, sweet and dill pickles and three kinds of salad dressing—French, blue cheese and mayonnaise. There was nothing they would not do to or put on a hamburger. The Easter Parade, if you can imagine it, was a burger and hot fudge between two pieces of untoasted white bread.

By the time I parked the car and went in, I knew what I wanted. My favorite, the Meet Me in St. Louis, which was a one-inch-thick burger, covered with bacon, tomato, Cheddar cheese, black olives, dill pickles and thousand island dressing, between two pieces of sourdough bread. I once asked Wally Slezak, the owner, if there was any connection between the ingredients and St. Louis and he said no because he had never personally been to St. Louis.

■

Jackie was already at the restaurant. I went over to the table, the one we always sat at in the far northwest corner. I sat down, we kissed.

And we immediately started talking about the murders. I told her everything I knew, which was what I had heard and seen at the Show, Tell and Pray meeting. I told her about going to see Jess Deaton and how I suspected, as I should have long before, that he had bribed The Cluck and the others to support Sooner Number One. I told her that made me as guilty of a crime as Jess Deaton was.

"That is absurd, Mack," she said. "Your crime, if it's even a crime, is believing people are as good and honest as you are."

"Honest and good people do not condone bribery."

"You are an honest man, Mack, the most honest there is in any government at any level in any state in any country on any planet there is in the universe."

"I winked while Jess bribed. I am sure of it. And I am just as sure that somehow that is connected to their having been killed."

"Well, Deaton's weird," she said. "Weird enough to do anything. I do not see what you see in that man. Comes back here out of nowhere with all of that money and starts throwing it around. I know, I know, he's thrown it at some good causes, some good ideas. But it's simply weird, Mack. It really is."

I was as tired of defending Jess as I was of defending Joe and as I was of most everything right then. So I changed the subject to Tommy Walt's demonstration and his request that I help him with Oklahoma Blue Arrow Motorcoaches.

"They're going to laugh, my dear Mack," she said. "Those bus people are going to laugh you all the way to Tulsa and back again on the Turner Turnpike five times."

Then a young waiter in a *Wizard of Oz* Tin Man suit was there with the loud, grim announcement: "There is an urgent phone call for you, Mr. Lieutenant Governor, from a Mr. Hayes. He said it was of the utmost urgency. Utmost. He said I should get you immediately."

Having just come off laughing about our eating out, I almost broke into another laughing fit as I walked to the phone. Okay, C. Who is number five? Another Democrat from the House? Or has the switch come to Republicans or the Senate or the welfare or highway commissioner? Who is number five? And how did he die? I know, I know. He was run over by an Oklahoma Blue Arrow bus powered by a mixture of methanol and old Somewhere Over the Rainbow Café hamburger grease.

C. said: "Come right now, Mack, to the fourth floor of the Federal Building. Get off the elevator, turn right and go to Room 412. I will meet you there."

"What's going on?" I asked.

"You wouldn't believe it if I told you," he said. "But please believe it's important enough to put off eating one of those silly cutesy hamburgers they sell there in that phony gyp joint.

Who in their right mind would ever pay seven-fifty for a hamburger with fudge on it?"

C. was a Burger King and McDonald's man.

"So, you are not telling me a fifth body has turned up?" I said.

"Not yet. Sorry to disappoint you."

I told him I would be right there and went back to the table to give Jackie the news.

"Be careful, Mack, that is all I ask," she said. "I do not want to be a widow again—particularly of the first lieutenant governor in history to ever die while conducting a murder investigation."

We kissed again and I left.

It was only after I was in the car and four or five blocks down May headed toward downtown that I realized she was still wearing her Chocolate Fork sash.

■

Buck Sporne was not like most FBI agents I had come across. He was still wearing a wide-lapeled light brown suit and a pair of highly polished red-brown cowboy boots that I had not noticed earlier. I hadn't paid that much attention before either to the fact that his blond hair, which he combed slicked back like he had just gotten out of the shower, was longer than the usual boot-camp cuts on most other FBI types. The skin on his tall, trim body—at least the part of it I could see—was a cracked tan, which with everything else helped him look a lot younger than his exhausted dark eyes showed him to be. Which was late forties or even early fifties.

Buck greeted me there in Room 412 of the Federal Building and introduced me to two other men who were identified as FBI agents. C. was the only other person present.

"You honor us with your presence, suh," said Buck to me in his charming drawl. "I regret our meeting had to happen on such short notice and so late at night. But I guess the taxpayers of our nation and state would say, 'That's what y'all hired on for, so hush.' "

It occurred to me at that second that there were probably hundreds of people in federal prisons all over America who had made the mistake of underestimating this cracker at one time or another.

Room 412 was a small windowless room with a pine conference table and eight matching chairs. There was a TV set and a VCR on a stand at one end of it.

"I think the best way to proceed, suh, is with the main attraction," said Buck, pointing me toward one of the chairs. "I think it is safe to say that the questions will flow naturally from that. Don't you agree, Brother Hayes?"

Brother Hayes nodded in agreement. C. had said nothing to me since I arrived nor had he done anything except look grave. This was clearly Buck Sporne's show.

Buck nodded to one of the other men, who leaned forward and switched on the TV set and VCR. Somebody cut the lights.

A grainy black-and-white shot of a room came on the TV screen. It was the living room at the town house in which The Cluck was killed.

After a few seconds, The Cluck entered. There was a buzzing sound. A doorbell, obviously. The Cluck, always a cluck, looked up at the camera that was taking this picture. "Here we go, J. Edgar, ready or not," he said, and gave a thumbs-up with his right hand.

He disappeared from view for a count of ten or so. And when he returned, another man was with him. It was Johnny Whistle.

They sat down and started talking.

"I am glad to see you have seen the light, Johnny," said The Cluck.

"There are always different lights to see at different times and places," said Johnny Whistle.

"Here's what we agreed on," said The Cluck. He handed Johnny a white business-size envelope. "Why don't you count it?"

Johnny Whistle opened the envelope and pulled out what looked like several dollar bills.

"Fifteen hundred was the price, right?" The Cluck said in a voice that was clearly meant to be heard and recorded.

"That's right," said Johnny Whistle. "It's all here."

"Did you say it was all here?" The Cluck said.

"That's right. Why are you talking so loudly?"

"Sorry. Right, sorry, Johnny."

"Jess Deaton's not going to like this one bit," Johnny Whistle said. He stood up.

"Well, we should never have gone with him in the first place."

"Seven hundred and fifty was hard to turn down," Johnny said. "I've got a kid in college and another going next year."

"You've got enough there to return it to him and still have it, if you get what I mean," said The Cluck.

"I get what you mean," said Johnny Whistle.

There was silence and the screen went blank.

I was stunned. And I was confused.

"What in the world does this mean?" I asked.

"First, it means we had an arrangement with the recently departed Representative Morgan," said Buck.

"What kind of an arrangement?" I asked.

"He was cooperating with us in an investigation."

I was slow but now I got it. And I could not believe it.

"The Cluck was a full-fledged idiot, a stupid fool, a clown."

"He was our clown," Buck said.

"You used him to bribe Johnny Whistle? Why? What in the world were you people up to?"

Buck nodded to the man up by the VCR and television set. "I regret to say we have another piece of tape to show you, Mr. Lieutenant Governor."

Again, the scene was the town house living room. Again, The

Cluck waved to the camera, left the room and returned with somebody. The somebody was the late State Representative Tipp Freeman of Ponca City.

"Whose money is it?" said young Freeman once they had sat down.

"What difference does it make as long as its good and its green?" said The Cluck.

"I don't take money, Jonah." Jonah. I had never heard anybody call The Cluck by his first name like that. "I do not take bribes."

I wished the camera had been closer. I wanted to see Freeman's face better. He sounded nervous and upset, but I could not see it well enough to make sure.

"You took one from that crazy pinko bastard Jess Deaton obviously," said The Cluck.

Freeman was on his feet. "I did not take money from him," he said in a voice hard to hear. The Cluck did not make him say it again or louder.

Freeman moved toward the door, and the sound and the picture again stopped.

■

Mostly for the next hour it was just Buck telling C. and me the incredible story of the FBI's Operation Broken Sooner Trust, a name that on first hearing resembled that of a small-town Oklahoma bank.

Buck said:

"It began, as we begin most of these governmental corruption stings, with one of our own agents, posing as a lobbyist of some kind, making an offer to one target. Our first target was Morgan. The approach was made in a town house which we had rented. Morgan accepted, and when he did we surprised him with the news that the man who had just bribed him was an undercover agent of the Federal Bureau of Investigation."

"Now, that's a tape I would love to see," I said.

"Some other day, Mr. Lieutenant Governor," Buck Sporne said, the smile still there but only barely. "Some other day."

"Sure," I replied, realizing that Buck, with all of his cracker charm, was an agent of the Federal Bureau of Investigation with a problem. A very, oh so very, serious problem.

"He agreed to approach other members of the legislature," said Buck. "We had just begun when . . . well, the dying started. Operation Broken Sooner Trust is now in a state of suspension."

I shook my head in wonder. I said: "Let me understand this. You bribed The Cluck—Jonah Morgan, to you—to change his position on Sooner Number One. You then used him to bribe Johnny Whistle to do the same. You tried to do the same thing on Freeman but he wouldn't play."

Buck nodded in agreement.

"Were there any others? Any others you bribed but have not died?"

"No, suh, there are not. As I said, our operation is under suspension. . . ."

"Do you understand, Mr. Sporne, how important Sooner Number One is to our state? Do you realize you were doing the devil's work?"

"Our interest was in their willingness to take money, not in the pros and cons of the issue itself," Buck said. "We are nonpartisan in our bribing, suh."

"That's an absurd way to go about things," said I. "Oklahoma needs that education program. For today, tomorrow and forever. Our children are being short-changed. Their futures and our state's future is being . . ."

C. broke in on me. "If it's all the same to you, Mack, if we could forget the speeches and concentrate now on another problem of today, tomorrow and forever. It's the one about the murder of members of the legislature. We're already at four and counting. I think you would agree Oklahoma needs a solution to that one, too."

"Okay, okay," I said. "But it is absolutely stupid to think the FBI, as long as it was going around bribing people, would not do it for just causes, for the right ideas."

"Frankly, Mr. Lieutenant Governor, we were not aware they had been bought in the first place by your friend, Mr. Deaton. If we had known that, we might have gone about it differently. We were operating only on some reliable information that some members of the Oklahoma legislature were susceptible to bribes. Our assignment was to test the assumption."

C. said: "You could have picked the names at random out of the legislature's phone book."

"That is not fair, C.," I said.

"Fair? Come on, Mack, please. You know and I know that it's conceivable the FBI could have ended up owning the whole goddamn legislature if it wanted to."

"That is an outrageous thing to say," I said. "There are some good and honest people in our legislature. I very much resent your blanket attack on a group of people . . ."

C. stopped me with his hands up over his head. "I promise no more blanket attacks, if you'll promise no more speeches." Then to Buck he said, "Since my friend Mack here made himself a folk hero with that great mummy speech in New York, he has had trouble not turning every little occasion into an oratory of some kind."

"I thought you were terrific in that speech, by the way," said Buck to me. "How's the search for the mummy going?"

"I take it the tape wasn't running for the murder of The Cluck?" I said quickly.

"You take it right on the money," Buck said. "Morgan wasn't doing anything for us at the time he was killed. Our people were not around."

Then I thought of something. Something that was missing. State Representative Doug Little of Pauls Valley was missing. I asked Buck Sporne about it.

"It's our only good news, suh. Our clown had not talked to Representative Little. He wasn't even on our list."

And then I thought of something else. Something sad and terrible. And more than obvious.

"Jess Deaton did the murders, didn't he?" I said directly to C.

"It sure looks that way, Mack," C. said. "I've asked Buck here to do a real and fast backgrounder on him. The one we did twelve years ago may have missed something."

"Can you prove it on Deaton?" Buck said.

"Nope. We have nothing. Not one thing. Not one single solitary piece of evidence. Not a hair, a speck of dust, a witness, nothing."

"Well, that is not completely so," said Buck Sporne. "We do have one more piece of tape that sure proves a little something relevant about your clown, the said Mr. Deaton."

He motioned again to the agent at the VCR.

The scene, once again, was the town house. The Cluck and Jess were sitting in the front room.

Jess said: "I hated to see you change your mind on Oklahoma Number One."

"Had to."

"Why?"

"It sucks."

"Sucks?"

"You know, sucks," said The Cluck, and then he made a sickening sucking sound with his mouth.

"You got a better offer, is that it?" Jess said. "Well, I will see it and double it."

"Look, Deaton, you know what I think of you. You are an egg-sucking left-wing sob sister with ideas that cost only money and that is that. I shouldn't have taken your money in the first place. I'll give it back to you. There is nothing you could say, no offer you could make, that would change my mind about a flea."

"Well, you know about fleas, that is for sure. They are your brothers, your like minds." Jess moved his body a bit in a way that made it clear he was about to get out of there.

"Don't talk superior because you ain't superior, Jess Deaton. Rich don't mean smart."

" 'The Cluck' is what they call you. Did you know that? Did you know that when the great minds of Oklahoma government discuss you they refer to you as The Cluck. Cluck as in dumb cluck. Did you know that, Jonah Morgan?"

Now The Cluck was on his feet.

Jess stood with him.

"Who paid you more?" Jess said. "That is all I want to know. Who's working the other side of the street? That is all I want to know."

"You'll be on the four o'clock Trailways to hell before you get that kind of information from me."

"I am already in hell. And now I am leaving hell."

He walked right out of the town house and the picture.

"Why didn't you tell me you had that?" C. asked.

"I just did, Mr. Director."

"Is it enough to prove Jess killed The Cluck?" I asked.

"It proves he knew somebody had turned his pigeons and that's important because it locks in the motive," C. said. "But it doesn't lock him into the killings themselves."

"I worry about how he found out about our project, to tell you the truth," said Sporne. "I really do worry about that because our security was, we thought, absolutely airtight."

"I've got so much to worry about now, I don't know where to begin," C. said, adding that he was going back to his office to do it, to see if anything new had turned up and to look at what little they did have through the new light of what we had just found out.

"You coming with me, Mack?"

No, I said. I was going home. We would talk first thing in the morning over breakfast.

"The usual time and place?"

"Why not?" I said.

■

C. got out of Room 412 in a hurry. I left a few moments later with Buck. We walked at a leisurely pace to the elevator. When we got there I realized that his associates had disappeared without a word.

"You mind walking me back to my hotel, Mr. Lieutenant

Governor?" he drawled. "I'm just around the corner at the Sheraton."

I did not mind. It was a dark, crisp, sweet night. The kind we in Oklahoma believed were given only to Oklahoma in October.

After we were outside on the sidewalk he got down to the business of the walk. "I guess it goes without saying how unusual it is for us of the Bureau to open up our business the way we have to you and to Brother Hayes," he said. "We normally play things so close to the vest, we burn holes in it."

"I understand," I said. I understood, too, that the choice was probably an easy one. Tell us and try to keep us quiet about what the FBI was doing. Don't tell us and risk us finding out on our own and having no obligation to keep it quiet.

"Can't you see the headlines on this one, suh?" he said. "TWO DEAD LEGISLATORS ON TAKE FROM FBI."

"Why didn't you tell C. all about it yesterday?" I asked. "Why did you wait?"

"I toyed with the idea of never telling him," Buck said. "That would have made me guilty of a crime, of withholding evidence in a murder. That would have made me as bad as the guys I go after. Worse, really. But the truth is, I seriously considered doing it. I really did. It was a close call. I really thought about folding my tent and getting the hell out of Oklahoma. I really thought about it."

"But you didn't. Good for you."

"No *goods* for me, suh. I deserve no *goods*. I almost crossed the line."

We crossed Kerr Avenue. There were no cars on the streets and no pedestrians on the sidewalks. There were seldom any of either anymore in downtown Oklahoma City after dark. It wasn't because it wasn't safe. It was because there wasn't anything for people to do down there. All of the big department stores, movie theaters and restaurants were long gone to malls and the suburbs. It was the single saddest thing about Oklahoma City, my lovely adopted city. It was only downtown in the daytime, when the banks and other office buildings and the courthouses were busy. At night you could not tell by looking the last time people were even there. Except at the two hotels that remained.

He popped the big question at the front door of the Sheraton.

"Can we look forward to some headlines or to some silence?"

"Well, from my point of view, I see no need for anything but silence right now," I said. "But that is only my view and there are others to consider."

"Could I offer you a bite to eat of your choice, suh?" said Buck. I was reminded of what C. always said about FBI agents. That they were the only people in his line of work he just automatically assumed were honest and fair until proven otherwise. With all the others he looked and sniffed for evidence before reaching that conclusion. His major complaints about them were that they were buttoned up and dull, and the one-mistake-and-you're-out atmosphere in which they worked made FBI agents extremely cautious. He said that was terrific when you were next to one in a shoot-out, but it also made them reluctant to take many risks. Buck, obviously, was an exception to a few of the rules.

And since I had had to skip my Meet Me in St. Louis Burger, and since I had gotten to like Buck Sporne, I took him up on supper.

The Sheraton coffee shop, as a matter of sad fact, was about the only eating place open downtown after eleven at night. The Park Plaza restaurant, which was fancy and French, closed at ten-thirty. The kitchen did, at least.

There was one burger on the Sheraton menu and it had a name: the Bud Wilkinson, after the former great OU football coach. I ordered it with fries and a diet Pepsi. Buck had a bowl of bean soup and a BLT with potato chips and a regular Pepsi.

"You ever go anywhere without your gun?" I asked Buck after a while of talking about nothing much of anything.

"Yes, suh," he said. "I only carry it now when I am definitely and for sure on duty. I used to wear it all of the time. I had this fear that I would be playing softball with the kids and suddenly across left field would walk some John Dillinger character and I couldn't do anything but go after him with a ball bat. But I eventually put that behind me. It was hard. Hard not to play FBI all of the time."

Our food came and we talked about the murders. He offered the serious possibility of their not being related. "I know the odds on such a thing are way up there, but so are they on the possibility of one killer using four different methods of killing.

The history on serial murders is that they do in their victims the same way every time. But this does not smell like your routine, everyday serial killer, does it?"

"I don't follow you," I said.

"Most mass killers are nutcake amateurs who stalk certain kinds or types of people—usually women—for nutcake reasons," Buck said as he sipped his soup, which had little hunks of ham in it and looked very good. "If these four were done by Deaton or any other same person, he or she is probably a sane pro."

"A sane pro?"

"Who else would have the expertise to pull off four different murders using four different methods?"

Buck asked me how I happened to become the lieutenant governor of Oklahoma. So I told him how I came to Adabel, Oklahoma, in the 1950s with my friend Tom Bell Pepper Bowen, how Pepper went off to the Korean War as a marine and was killed, how I then married Jackie, his widow. Then how I was elected county commissioner, and, after I fought successfully to have a statue of a Korean War veteran built on the courthouse lawn, how I was picked by the Democratic state committee as a "fresh face" to run with Buffalo Joe as lieutenant governor. I left out a few things here and there, but I had the feeling watching him listen that he already knew the story. My father, the retired Kansas highway patrolman, used to say a good cop is the one who knows the answer to every question he asks before he asks it. Lawyers say the same thing about good lawyers.

We had moved to coffee and pecan pie when I began asking him about himself. He said he had been an FBI agent for twenty-four years, most of the time working in California. He now lived in Washington and specialized in what he called "government corruption matters."

"This is the first time I've had any of my people murdered," he said, "much less three of them in twenty-four hours."

I realized that C. and I, for the moment, owned this charming man. His future was in our hands. We could ruin it all for him. But I also knew that no matter what C. and I did, someday it would get out. Someday the world would know about the fact that the FBI was operating a sting that somehow got some members of the Oklahoma legislature murdered. Somehow. It reminded me of how fine the line is sometimes between good and evil.

I also knew that Buck Sporne was smart enough to know that all he was bargaining for with me was time. Time for C. to find out what happened so the story could all be told at one time.

"How did you happen to choose a career in the FBI?" I asked. It was not an idle question. I had always been fascinated by how people ended up doing what they were doing.

He looked at me, smiled and gave me an answer like none I had ever gotten before.

"I grew up in a small town in south Georgia named Beeville. 'To Get Stung by Beeville Is to Be Stung for Life' was our town motto. My mother taught algebra, geometry and trigonometry in our high school. Dad taught science and biology and coached

football and basketball. Our teams were called the Beeville
Hornets. Dad was also in show business on the side, as a hobby.
He was Ken Sporne the Pop Bottle Man. He was the best in the
world because he was the only one. What he did was stack
empty pop bottles. He started with RCs—Royal Crown colas.
He'd put them one on top of the other, upside down, longwise
and all. He made them into designs. Cars, trucks, train engines,
buildings, churches—things like that. He had started doing it
as a kid and one day the owner of a carnival asked him to do
it before a crowd. That was where his performing started. In a
matter of minutes he could take a hundred or so bottles and,
like magic, turn them into something. Then dismantle it and
make something else. He never broke a bottle. Never. His
mightiest achievement was a medieval castle. More than two
hundred RC bottles were in it, and when he was done somebody glued them all together in place. It still exists and is on
display Monday through Friday in the lobby of the public
library in Macon as we speak."

Buck Sporne, son of Ken Sporne the Pop Bottle Man, had
some more pie and a sip of coffee. And continued.

"The problem after a while was that he got to liking traveling with carnivals more than he did living at home with us and
teaching and coaching the Beeville Hornets. He also got successful. One day a guy from Pepsi-Cola came along and asked
him why he didn't use Pepsi bottles instead of RCs. Then there
was a regional rep for Grapette and two guys from Dr Pepper
and another from Nesbitt's. Dad, who was no dummy, had
himself a little bidding war. Every few months he would

change the brand names of the bottles he used according to who won the bidding. But that's not important. The important thing was that one Sunday night he didn't come back from the carnival, which was playing in Savannah that weekend. He called Mom instead and said he was never coming back. He said he was made for a life on the road in show business and that was that. I was fourteen at the time and I am now fifty-one and I have not laid eyes on him since."

"So it was to find him that you later joined the FBI?" I asked.

Buck laughed at that idea. And he shook his head and his blue eyes got darker and sadder. "No, no, suh. It was nothing like that. It was two years later, when I was sixteen, that I came home from football practice one afternoon late and two men in coats and ties were there talking to my mom. I came in and Mom told me they were with the FBI and she told them that I was the man of the house so they could go on talking in front of me. One of the agents said they were looking for a man who just might be my father who just might be responsible for driving a getaway car for a gang of bank robbers in Alabama. They asked some questions about my father and some dates and it became clear that the man they wanted was probably not my father. The important thing was that I walked outside with the two agents. They had a slick dark blue four-door Ford sedan outside. The agents were both men in their thirties who looked like they could wrestle gators to the ground. They were terrifically nice to me, and when they drove away I decided right then and there that I would be one of them someday. I would be an FBI agent. Dumb kind of thing, wasn't it, when you think about it? Be around two men for a few minutes when you are sixteen and make a life's decision because of it. Just like that."

I told him I didn't think it was dumb at all. And I asked him if he ever tried later to find out anything about his father.

"I almost did," he said. "My mother died of stomach cancer four years ago, and after I came back to Washington from Georgia and the funeral I went down to our big National Crime Records computer room. I wrote my dad's name on a piece of paper all set to give it to one of our guys with the request to run a name check. It would tell me if my father had ever been arrested and all the rest. But at the last second I crumpled up the paper and threw it away. I decided I didn't want to know. Maybe someday I will. Maybe. I just don't know. He's probably dead from all that travel by now anyhow. Who knows?"

It made me know how lucky I was to have had my Trooper Dad, a Kansas highway patrolman, as my father.

And it reminded me of the fact that with so much going on in my life I had not talked to him in a while. How long had it been? Three weeks? No, four weeks at least. That was too long.

■

Jackie was in bed, under the covers and asleep, when I got home. She always woke up barely when I came in late like that and she did again. In her most half-asleep voice she asked: "Are you safe?"

"I am, thank you," I replied.

"Channel ten said that city marshal in Davidson was about to die."

"Too bad," I said.

"They also said your girlfriend Sandra Faye Parsons got another mummy in the mail. Good night."

And I heard the sound of a kiss.

Sandra Faye Parsons was the woman of the mummies, the director of the Oklahoma Historical Society's Museum of the Cherokee Strip in Enid. She was not my girlfriend. I had no girlfriends, not now, not ever since I married Jackie. I had very few even before that.

I was going to have to go see Sandra Faye Parsons and do something about the mummy problem. I could not ignore her and her problem much longer. I really could not.

I remembered the note she had sent and made a mental note to open and read it sometime soon.

It took me ten minutes or so to get on my pajamas and otherwise get ready for bed. It wasn't until I was in bed with the light off and snuggled up next to her that I noticed Jackie was wearing her Chocolate Fork sash over her nightgown.

I kissed her on the neck, as was my custom at times and occasions such as this.

"I'm going to wear my sash everywhere I go," she said after a count of seven.

"People are going to think it's strange everywhere you go," I said after a count of one and a half.

"I don't care."

"It's like Billy Sims walking around with a sign saying he's a football star. Tommy Walt's embarrassed about it."

"Tommy Walt's embarrassed? Well, well, bless his heart. He's sure one to talk. I don't collect restaurant grease for a living. He does."

I thought that was a very good point, particularly when I remembered my promise to see the boys at Oklahoma Blue Arrow in the morning about letting him pour old restaurant grease down the gas tanks of their buses.

■

I couldn't go to sleep. So after a while I got up and went to the kitchen and called my father. It was after midnight, but I knew he would be up. He got by on four hours' sleep and was seldom even near his bed before one A.M.

"Son!" he boomed. He always boomed and he always called me "Son." Never "Mack," my made-up name. Never my real one either. Always simply "Son." It was never a problem because I was the only one he had. The only other person in the family was my sister, who was now married and lived in Topeka. Dad, a captain in the Kansas Highway Patrol, was commander of the patrol detachment in Hays, which was in western Kansas 120 miles west of Salina. My mother had died when I was twelve years old from appendicitis, something hardly anybody ever dies from anymore.

My father had a radio announcer's voice, a doctor's gentleness and the posture and character of a monument. I loved him very much. I had grown up wanting only to be like him, only to be a Kansas highway patrolman just like him. It was my trooper dream for my life that ended when I lost my eye when I was sixteen and half years old. I was watching some kids play kick the can and somebody kicked a can up in my face.

"What's up, Dad?" was all I said to him. It was all I ever had to say to him.

"I'm thinking about adopting me a baby," he said. "That's what's up."

And I listened to the story of how he and a young trooper were out on the interstate—I-70—between Russell and Bunker Hill when they came upon a car parked on the shoulder. It looked abandoned. They pulled up behind it and walked up to it and discovered there was a young woman in the front seat screaming at the top of her lungs, "It's coming! My baby's coming!"

Dad said she was bleeding badly and she was crying and losing consciousness from time to time. He told the young trooper to run back to their car and radio for an ambulance.

But before an ambulance or anybody else came, the baby was born.

"I delivered the baby, Son. It was my seventeenth, if I have counted correctly." In thirty-two years as a Kansas trooper, my dad, Trooper Dad, had delivered babies along the sides of roads, in living rooms, service-station rest rooms and similar places. He had an album full of their photographs and their letters as they grew up and their parents kept him informed about their lives.

"Congratulations, Dad."

"No, Son. No congratulations this time. I lost her."

"The baby?"

"No, the mother. She died right there in the front seat of the car before I could do anything about it. The doctors said afterward that she had some kind of infection up there that she had not seen about. The baby's a real pistol."

"Boy?"

"Yep. Want him? There's no daddy or any other relative around we can find. The papers are calling him Trooper Baby. He'd do great in the family of the lieutenant governor of Oklahoma. You could call him Mack Two."

"No thanks, Dad. You're not really thinking of doing anything stupid yourself like adopting . . ."

"I'd love to, but I'm too old and too alone and they'd never let me. Gave you a start, though, didn't I, Son?"

"Yes, sir."

We talked for another thirty or forty minutes about my problems with the mummies and the murders and Digger Donnelly and some of the difficulties he was having with some of the younger troopers.

"They're different these days, Son. They want to be cops, but they also want to be everything else, too."

I didn't know what he meant and it did not matter.

He asked about Jackie and I told him about the silly Chocolate Fork sash.

"Leave her alone about it, Son," he said.

"Dad, she's making a fool of herself."

"That's why you've got to leave her alone. Making a fool of yourself is one of our most precious rights. Right up there with being allowed to have a lawyer and make a phone call when you're arrested."

"I'm telling you, Dad, she's acting like a fool."

"Better to act like one than be one, Son."

I loved my dad.

He asked if I wanted him to come down and give us a hand on the legislators murder case. I told him, no thanks.

"I wish somebody would do something like that up here," he said.

"Like what?"

"Kill off a few of our state legislators. I could give them a few names for starters."

I loved my dad. I was so glad I had called him.

Chapter 4

The worst thing about my friend C. Harry Hayes was the way he ate. He simply could not do it without dripping catsup, chow mein juice, salsa, raspberry preserves or whatever was available on him, his clothes and those around him. And since we often had lunch or breakfast together, that often meant me. He was otherwise a neat and tidy man in his dress, bearing and thinking. But there was something about food that caused him to spill and drip.

"Could it have something to do with having only one ear?" I said to him now as he wiped a glob of orange marmalade off the lapel of his gray suit coat. He almost always wore gray because that was almost the only color of the suits, sport coats and slacks he owned. He said it cut down the number of decisions he had to make when dressing in the morning. Gray also matched his skin coloring and his tall, thin personality.

"Watch out with that talk or I'll turn our friends in the crip lobby loose on you and your black eye patch," he said.

His one-earedness and my one-eyedness were among the things that made us friends and kept us that way. He lost an ear in a firing-range accident when he was a young cop in Durant. But the other things between us, like trust and fun, were more important. We had collaborated on several adventures in the course of doing what we thought was in the best interest of the people of Oklahoma. Usually we did it quietly in private, but sometimes we did it openly and publicly, like now, in trying to solve what all of the papers and the people on television were calling the Capitol Ripper Murders.

We had gone through the drive-through at Oklahoma Red Dog Heaven #5 on North May. Since C. and I first became friends and started having meals together—mostly lunch but occasionally breakfast—we usually ate in the backseat of his Lincoln Town Car command car while one of his agent-drivers chauffeured us around the streets of Oklahoma City. The food was always fast food, which we acquired from drive-through lines. We began alternating between McDonald's and Wendy's, but as time went on he insisted on frequenting other places as well. There were flings with tacos, with barbecue, with Chinese, with pizza, with fried chicken and biscuits. We then went back to the McDonald's/Wendy's mode for a while and started down the list again. Now, at my suggestion, we were trying hot dogs. I loved corny dogs, and the Oklahoma Red Dog chain had the best in Oklahoma City and had just recently initiated a whole new line of things for breakfast.

I had a corny dog omelet, which was an omelet wrapped around a corny dog, with an order of home fries and a tall glass of orange juice. He had what they called a Scrambled Dog, which was a plate of scrambled eggs doctored with pieces of hot dog and chili and flavored with grated cheese, onions and mustard. He also had a cup of black coffee and a glass of milk.

He told me what I already suspected. There was nothing new. There was nothing the OBI or the OCPD had that could tie Jess Deaton to any of those killings.

"All we have is a motive that those FBI tapes make obvious for all to see," he said.

"That seems kind of drastic," I said. "Sooner Number One is important, but to kill people over it seems over the line."

C. said: "While you were in Chicago with Jackie and her apple screwdrivers or whatever, we had a guy over in Pawhuska kill his next-door neighbor because he wouldn't take down a clothes line. The clothes line had underwear on it and the guy found that offensive to his wife and daughters. They got into it and he blew the guy away with a twelve-gauge."

"I follow you . . ."

"You remember what happened in Adabel, your old hometown, last year. The coach of the junior high school basketball team poisoned the coach of the junior high school basketball team in Mineola to help level things out for the state play-offs."

"Now, that I could understand. . . ."

"Don't forget the Wal-Mart clerk in Ardmore who was strangled to death by a farmer who claimed she gave him change for a ten-dollar bill instead of a twenty."

"Okay, okay . . ."

"What about your friend, that Trailways bus driver, who

drove a whole load of passengers off the Red River bridge north of Dennison so he could kill his girlfriend and himself."

"He wasn't my friend. But I get it. I really do get it. People kill one another for stupid and small reasons. I get it, C."

"I happen to believe that killing is too easy and too acceptable to everybody," said C., winding up doing exactly what he accused me of being too prone to do, which was making a speech at the drop of a bite of scrambled egg, one of which had just landed on his tie, which was black with small white stripes running through it at an angle. "That's why murder is named in the Ten Commandments, Mack. That's how the West was won. That's why there are cops like me. It's common and the reasons for it are common."

"What are we going to do about Jess, is the question." I was not up to a speech on murder, thank you.

"My guess is that we're going to find that killing people is more than common and acceptable to Jess Deaton. That is my guess."

"That is not an answer to my question."

"We haven't got enough to arrest him. Not by a long shot. You got any ideas, Mr. One-eyed Mack, you feel free to spit them out."

I had a mouth full of my omelet right then. I spit out nothing.

"You like Jess Deaton, don't you?" C. asked. "You have trouble seeing him as a killer?"

"Yes, to both questions."

"I have been around several hundred killers in my life,

Mack. I never ever met one who looked or talked like one. They all talked and looked like you and me and that kid in the drive-through who gave us our breakfast and the guy who put hot dogs in the scrambled eggs back there in the kitchen and the woman driving that Ford pickup next to us now. She could be on the way to killing her boyfriend or her boss or her momma or a complete stranger right now."

We were stopped at a red light at the corner of Sixty-third Street and Meridian. The woman in the truck was pretty, about twenty-two. Her hair was up in rollers and there was a baby in a car seat next to her. I figured she had just taken her husband to work somewhere and was now on her way back home to spend her day as a momma. She did not look like she was on her way to kill somebody.

"I get it, C.," I said.

"The line between good and evil is about as thin as the one down the center of these eggs," he said.

I looked down at his Scrambled Dog. There was no line to be seen down the center of them or anything else on his plate. It was just an awful-looking mess of eggs with little hunks of things in it.

He reminded me of the time Jess Deaton came to see him with his suitcase and offered to buy him a new Lincoln command car if he moved a regional OBI office to Diamond Grove. C. decided to look the other way because of all the good things Deaton was doing for his town and its people.

"Which was worse, him offering the bribe or me not arresting him for doing it?" C. asked. "Fine lines are everywhere, Mack."

I know fine lines are everywhere, C.

We were barely through the intersection when a large blue Chrysler swerved in front of us. I recognized the car immediately as the official car of the governor. I recognized immediately that it was Joe who was waving furiously at us from the backseat.

His car stopped, we stopped right behind him. Before either of us could get out of our car, Joe was there at my door. He threw it open and said: "Move over. I am here on official business. Official business. Move over."

I moved over to the center of the backseat, squashing up against C. and causing him to spill some of his Scrambled Dog on the front of his pants. "Sorry," I said.

"Get him out of here," Joe said, pointing to the OBI agent–driver in the front seat.

"Wait for us outside," C. said to the agent, who did as he was told. He got out of the car.

"Did you see this? Did either of you pieces of dog ___ see this?" Joe yelled.

He stuck the front page of the *Daily Oklahoman* in front of us. I had indeed seen it before I left the house and I was sure C. had, too. There was no way to miss the *Daily Oklahoman* in Oklahoma City.

There was a full one-inch-high banner headline across the top of the page. WHO WILL BE NEXT TO FALL TO THE RIPPER?

it screamed. Under it were large portrait shots of The Cluck, Freeman, Little and Whistle with a light check mark through each of their faces.

The story quoted all kinds of people, including the police chief of Oklahoma City, several members of the legislature and even some preachers, expressing fear about what might be still to come from the reign of terror inflicted on the people of Oklahoma by the Capitol Ripper, whoever and whatever he or they may be.

Joe pointed at a paragraph down the page. He read out loud: "Republican state chairman Clay (Sonny) Malone said: 'The real question is where is the governor? He put the lieutenant governor in charge of the worst plague to hit the state in its history and disappears. Where are you, Buffalo Joe? Come out, come out, wherever you are.' Chairman Malone is rumored to be considering challenging Governor Hayman in next year's election."

"What have you done to me?" Joe screamed. "What have you done?"

His head was turned in my direction, but I had no idea who he meant. Did he mean Sonny Malone?

"And it's in this paper! This ___ ___ paper!"

There was nothing to say. At least I had nothing to say. I hoped and prayed C. saw it the same way.

Joe hated the *Daily Oklahoman* and the *Daily Oklahoman* hated him. Seldom an edition went by in which he was not attacked or molested on its editorial page. It was mostly because the *Daily Oklahoman,* like so many people in our state, was basically against all governments at all levels and everyone involved in all governments at all levels. Joe knew that, but he still took every thing the *Oklahoman* said about him very personally. In fact, he took all criticism that way. "Personal is the only kind of criticism there is, Mack," he explained. "That's the reason I take it that way."

"I'm sorry, Joe," I said. "Maybe next time we should play it differently. . . ."

"Next time? Next time? There had better not be a next time! No, Mack. No more next times! None! Zero! This murder wave is over! Now! Right now as of now! Do you hear me, Mack?"

I told him I heard him.

I dared not look over at C. I dared not think about what C. was probably on the verge of saying either.

Joe said: "I want you to issue a statement immediately saying you are on the verge of arresting the Capitol Ripper. I want you to say the case was cracked because of the leadership you received from the governor. I want that done immediately." He looked directly at C.'s and my breakfasts, still in our laps and getting cold. "For a few minutes I want you to put aside the mundane things of life such as eating to do the people's work, to put out a press statement. I want it done, and I want it done now."

I had a decision to make. A decision that, for all the reasons that are now very obvious, could cost me my place in the Hayman-Mack administration, my job as Second Man of Oklahoma.

Speaking ever so gently, I said: "That would be a lie, Joe. I could not do that. That would be wrong."

Joe leaned out from the seat and directed his first words directly to C. "You ever lied for a greater good, Hayes? Is a greater good worth a lie, Mr. Director?"

"Is the governor aware of the so-called Nuremberg rule?" C. responded in that phony third-person way members of legislative bodies often referred to themselves during floor debates.

Joe picked up on the game and played. "Yes, the governor is, as a matter of fact. It says a person has a responsibility to refuse to obey an illegal or immoral order. Something like that. Is it the something-like-that the director was referring to?"

"Precisely," C. said.

"So the director is saying lying to some two-bit reporter is the same as sending millions of people to their deaths in ovens? Is that what the director is saying to the governor? Is that really what he is saying? Because if it is, then the director is out of his mind. The director is a ___ ___ fool."

"The governor is the ___ ___ fool," C. said.

"I do not like you, sir," Joe said.

"I do not like you, sir," C. said.

Joe opened the car door. He said, in his public-announcement mode:

"Mack, you and your insubordinate cow-___, cat-___, pig-___, dog-___ friend the director here have twenty-four hours to crack this thing. If by this time tomorrow you have not found and arrested the person or persons responsible for these crimes against the order and decency of our state, then I will personally take charge."

"And do what?" said C. with contempt.

"Call a news conference."

"Boy, that'll show 'em. Stand by, Ripper! Here comes the governor with a news conference!"

Ignoring C., Joe replied, as if he were announcing a state of war with Arkansas: "I'll call it for the two of you to answer questions about how the investigation is going."

"You are the complete, ultimate idiot," C. said. "The most complete, the most ultimate in the history of this or any other state."

"One of these days you are a goner, Hayes. One of these days you will look up and this car and that office of yours and that badge and swagger you wear will be a goner."

Joe, in fact, had tried several times to fire C. But each time the legislature and the other law-enforcement people in the state forced him to back down—and off.

Now he got out of the car, took a step away and then returned. He tapped on the window and motioned for me to roll it down.

He held up the paper again. Below the fold and down in the right-hand corner of the front page was another story I had already seen and read. It was about Marshal Digger Don Donnelly of Davidson. Doctors said he would not last more than a few more days if he did not eat. Digger was quoted for the thousandth time saying he was prepared to die for his cause.

"If I die it will be on the conscience of the legislature and the governor and the lieutenant governor of this state for the rest of their lives. Particularly the governor, that fool Hayman. It might be worth dying just to give him a fit or two."

"I told you to take care of it, Mack," Joe said.

"I will," I said.

Joe was gone again.

"Take over, Mack," C. said once the window was back up. "Go with me now to a lunacy court judge and ask to be that man's official guardian and keeper. Go to the legislature or the Supreme Court or to McDonald's or Sears Roebuck or to a Conoco or wherever you have to go to take over our state before it is too late. Do not let one more day go by with that ___ ___ fool idiot running things. Please, Mack. For the good of us all, Mack. I beg of you, I implore you. I will strangle you with an orange and black O. State Cowboys ribbon if you do not."

There was Joe again at my car window. I rolled it down again. He leaned his head in.

"Just for the record of life, my two missing-one-thing friends, let me tell you something before I leave. Let me tell you that I know how the two of you and the two of others there and here and everywhere like to make fun of me, like to say things that would make people believe I am peculiar, strange, weird, different—even crazy.

"Well, let me tell you that there is nothing I do, have done or will do that is more peculiar, strange, weird, different—even crazy—than sitting in the backseat of a car like the two of you with plates of runny eggs in your laps. Normal, healthy people do not do that, gentlemen. Normal, healthy people eat breakfast at tables in their homes with their families or at restaurants sitting in chairs. Let me tell you that before you go about your business of laughing or poking fun or being smart-mouthed about me and my way of doing things and life.

"Remember what I have always said to you, Mack. A man who can't look at himself in the mirror can't see the real himself."

I didn't remember his ever telling me that.

"If you two missing-one-of-something freaks could look at yourselves sitting there now, I swear to the God in Sooner heaven that you would see the real himselfs of both of you. And it would not be a pretty or sane sight."

He was gone again. I rolled up the car window again.

"He's absolutely right, you know," I said to C.

C. said nothing. He put a bite of Scrambled Dog in his mouth as our car moved away from the curb. A small piece of the egg slipped from the right side of his mouth and fell harmlessly on the top of his right hand.

"Good catch," I said.

■

Jackie had called it right. The boys at Blue Arrow laughed. And laughed and laughed.

We were in the office of Bill Hylton, Oklahoma Blue Arrow's president and general manager out off West Reno Avenue. He did an impression of a carnival barker. "Step right up! Fry your hot dogs while seeing Oklahoma on a Blue Arrow bus!" Larry Reese, the Blue Arrow general passenger agent, had some difficult things to say about Tommy Walt.

"I cannot imagine how he could stomach using his precious old restaurant grease in an engine of something so awful as an intercity bus," said Reese.

Reese remembered. Everyone remembered. Tommy Walt could not stand putting baggage checks on suitcases or writing up waybills on package express. He also could not deal with the fact that baggage and express got lost for no apparent reason. A porter would put a suitcase on a nonstop bus to Tulsa and the bus would arrive without the suitcase. One day he went a little crazy and wrote awful words on the walls of the men's room at the bus depot. I interceded and he was given a second chance. After a while he lost control of himself again. This time he threw a suitcase through a plate-glass window and ran away. I interceded again.

"No, no," I said to Reese. "He loved buses, he still loves buses. He just was not up to the pressure of the work."

"Pressure? Pressure of taking a cardboard baggage check, tearing off one half of it across a perforated line, giving half of it to the passenger and tying the other half to a suitcase? Get serious, Mack. You have raised a son who hates buses. Why can't you just accept and live with it?"

Reese and Hylton were both in their middle to late forties.

Both had started as bus drivers and worked their way up and around the company. Both were short-haired, well groomed and overweight. Both loved buses even more than I did.

"Well, it doesn't matter," I said. "This is business. All he's asking for is a chance to have a demonstration. What have you got to lose?"

Hylton, still smiling, said: "What we have to lose, Mack, is the engine of every bus we pour grease into. Who knows what that old stuff could do to a diesel engine?"

"Make it smell like fried onions for starters," Reese said.

"I saw a demonstration on a Mercedes," I said. "He and this professor did it. It fired up just great. I promise you I saw it with my own one good eye."

"Did you go back to the tailpipe?" Reese asked.

"No, why?"

"To see if it smelled like fried chicken, Burger Kings or whatever."

Hylton, an old friend, finally said: "Have Tommy Walt call me. We've got an old Jimmy diesel out back on which we can at least let him do a demonstration. But that is it, Mack. I mean, it."

Jimmy was what truck and bus people called GMCs.

"Thanks, Bill." I shook his hand warmly.

And then, as they had promised when I arrived, they took me next door to their garage to see their newest bus. It was an MC-9 that had just been driven in from the factory in Roswell, New Mexico. The MCI was Greyhound's top-of-the-line inter-city coach. It had forty-nine reclining seats, a rest room, an automatic shift, a Detroit diesel engine and everything you could ever want in a bus. This one was particularly sparkling and beautiful in its Oklahoma Blue Arrow livery—white base with two huge blue arrows that started with their individual points in the center of the bus's front and then swept down each side to come together again across the rear with their matching feathered heads.

Admiring her, touching her, walking through her, smelling her, almost made the visit a pleasure.

I went from the bus garage directly to I-44 West for the fifty-minute drive to Davidson to what I was sure would be a real nonpleasure—seeing Digger Donnelly.

■

I found him in a cot in his office at city hall, a two-room white wooden building on Davidson's main street. It was the main street and only one of three paved streets in the town of 650 or so Sooners. There were several of them crowded around the cot attending to Digger. One of them had on a coat and tie and introduced himself to me as a doctor.

"He's getting worse and worse," he said.

It was something I did not have to be told. Digger, who, I knew from the newspapers, was thirty-seven years old, looked twice that. There were big black rings under his eyes, which were blue and fallen back into his head. His skin was tissue-white, his blond hair uncombed and greasy.

Somebody put a chair by the cot for me to sit in. Digger's head was turned away from me, facing a wall. The wall was made of a false dark-wood paneling. There was a calendar from a fire extinguisher supply company in Tulsa pinned up there. It was turned to October, which featured a black-and-white picture of an antique fire engine.

"Digger," I said. "It's me, Mack, the lieutenant governor."

"Screw you," I thought he said, but I wasn't sure. He did not move his head toward me and spoke in a barely audible whisper.

"You're about to die, Digger, for a cause that doesn't mean anything. Die for freedom or democracy or life, liberty and the pursuit of happiness. Not for the right to give speeding tickets."

"Screw you and your mummies," I thought he said.

"In fact, you can still give out the tickets, Digger. You just can't keep all of the money. Isn't it fair that the state get some of it to fix the roads and highways and bridges? Fairness is all that is at issue here. You're a fair man. Be fair."

"Screw you and your New York speech," I was fairly sure he said.

"How did you get the name 'Digger'?" I asked.

Digger moved his head to face me. He smiled. "I played fullback in high school. Linebacker on defense. I dug in when I ran, I dug in when I tackled. I was a digger. Digger Don Donnelly. Have you ever heard of me?"

"You bet I have," I said, telling a lie for a greater good. "Nobody in the history of sports in our state has ever dug in like you. And here you are doing it again."

"I played fullback on offense, linebacker on defense. I dug in both ways. I mean, I tore into that dirt. Those cleats of mine tore holes in that dirt. I played fullback on offense, linebacker on defense."

"Don't die in the name of speeding tickets, Digger. Don't get that on your tombstone. You want Digger on there. You want it to say, 'He played fullback on offense, linebacker on defense and he dug in both ways.' If you die over speeding tickets, it isn't going to say anything about digging in. Not a word. It's going to say something about speeding tickets. 'Here lies the only man in the history of Oklahoma and the world to give his life for the unrestricted right to give speeding tickets.' That is not the same, Digger."

He sat up suddenly. "I'm Digger. You can't make me not be Digger." His voice was clear. And almost normal.

"Nobody wants to," I said. "Only you can do that to yourself."

"I hate politicians," he said, still clear, still almost normal.

"So do I," I said.

"Aren't you one of 'em?"

"No, sir. Not me. I hate 'em as much as you do. I am a lieutenant governor. Lieutenant governors can't be politicians or they wouldn't be lieutenant governors. They'd be governors. . . ."

"Joe the Buffalo is the worst politician. Do you hate him?"

"He's the governor, Digger, I'm the lieutenant governor. He's number one, I'm number two. I can't hate him. It's against the Constitution."

"What is a lieutenant governor?" he asked.

"A messenger, Digger. A lieutenant governor is a messenger of hope and life. . . ."

"Messager?"

"Messenger."

"Will you help me screw the politicians?"

"You bet I will."

He closed his eyes and lay back down. All his strength was gone. His voice went back to a whisper. The doctor, the others and I leaned over to hear him say:

"Get me a cheeseburger with fried onions, lettuce, tomato and mayo. Also some fries with ketchup, a plate of spaghetti with chili, a short stack with melted butter and hot maple syrup, a glass of chocolate milk and a Bud. And a large piece of chocolate layer cake with chocolate twirl ice cream, a whole pecan pie and a peach. Washed. I want that peach washed clean."

The other people in the room, including a woman I had not noticed until now, began to clap and cry and say "Hallelujah." And shake my hand in gratitude.

"You did it, Mack," said somebody. "You made a miracle, you saved a life worth saving," said another.

It was one of my finest moments as lieutenant governor of Oklahoma.

It made me feel so good, I decided to return to Oklahoma

City by way of Diamond Grove, which was only a few miles and minutes out of the way.

■

Jess Deaton's town of Diamond Grove had a population of 12,500. He grew up there, left after high school to go to a college in some eastern place like Massachusetts and did not come back until a hot August day forty-two years later. Nobody was there to meet or greet him because his parents, his brother and all of his family were either dead or moved away and there was nobody else around who much remembered him. He did not tell anybody where he had been or what he had been doing or how he got rich.

C. was asked by the sheriff down there to run a check on Jesse Albert Deaton to see if he was a dope dealer, a runaway bank president or something else bad. The check turned up nothing. The sheriff spread the word that Jess was clean and the people of Diamond Grove and Jess Deaton went on to know and love each other. He bought a small house in town, then a whole block of vacant houses, then the dying dry-goods store, a dying bank, then two blocks of dying downtown, all the vacant lots in town and on and on until he mostly owned all of Diamond Grove. His last major buy was the Diamond Grove Hammer Company, the only hammer factory west of St. Louis and the town's major employer.

The main thing he spent his money on, though, was teachers and books and other things for the Diamond Grove schools. He paid the recruitment and extra salary costs to hire Ph.D.'s in science and English and history to teach in the elementary, junior high and high schools. He set up funds for them to take extra college courses and sabbaticals. Every student who finished high school was guaranteed a college education. Every Diamond Grove kid who got a college degree was guaranteed a job back in Diamond Grove. The *Daily Oklahoman* called it "something that smells a lot like socialism." The people of Diamond Grove called it something wonderful.

I arrived in Diamond Grove in my Skylark that afternoon just after three right in the middle of a big public ceremony in front of city hall. Jess was up there on a small stage doing his favorite thing—handing out money. But it was all perfectly legal and delightful. He was there in his khakis giving checks to twenty-seven Diamond Grove kids who had dropped out of high school for a year or more and then gone back and graduated. The checks were for ten thousand dollars each.

"No strings attached," Jess told them between coughs. "If you now go on to college, I will pay all of your expenses as long as you maintain a C average. But if you do nothing more than this that is fine, too. The ten thousand dollars is yours to spend as you wish on what you wish. Congratulations. I'm proud to know you."

It was another October magic day. The sun was there, and when it was on you directly it was hot, but under a cottonwood or a sycamore it was cool. There were at least three hundred people standing out in front of the little stage where Jess, the twenty-seven honorees and some important-looking other people were.

Everyone cheered for Jess. The Diamond Grove High School orchestra, called the Strings of Diamond Grove, played "For He's a Jolly Good Fellow."

Then one of the twenty-seven winners came up to the microphone. She was a black girl in a pink dress who looked to be about nineteen or twenty years old. She was tall, handsome, striking, even though her hair was done up in what looked like twenty-five or thirty tiny little braids, which I assumed was something African. When she started talking I understood why she had won something. Her voice was deep and resonant, more like a young man's than a young woman's.

"Thank you, Mr. Deaton," she boomed. "Thank you from the bottom of our hearts—and our pocketbooks. The system pretty much gave up on us, sir. But you didn't. You said, 'Try again, work a little harder, try a little harder, and you will be rewarded.' You spoke, we heard, we did it and you did it. Thank you, Mr. Deaton. I for one am going on to college. I heard that, too. I am going on and on to Southeastern State and then on and on some more and I am going to always remember you, Mr. Deaton. They call us Deaton Scholars. We ain't scholars. We're just lucky to have grown up here in Diamond Grove where you are, Mr. Deaton."

I had the certain feeling that I had just heard from somebody who was going to go on and on to be very important in the world of Oklahoma someday. She could even end up as the first black and first woman lieutenant governor of Oklahoma.

Jess, who never seemed pleased to see me, seemed even less than usual. I caught him as he came down from the platform.

"That was wonderful, Jess. It really was," I said.

"If you politicians did your jobs, then it wouldn't be necessary for people like me to clean up after your messes," he said. And he coughed into his handkerchief. "What do you want with me?"

"I want to talk to you about the murders."

He waved his handkerchief at me as if I were a fly. But I did not buzz away.

"There's something really weird going on, Jess. I need your help."

"Weird? What's weird about killing some people who needed killing?"

"Come on, you old fool. Talk to me. Talk to me about all of this."

He looked at me and the look asked a question. "No, C. did not put a wire on me," I said. "You can check me if you want."

C. not only had not wired me for sound, he did not even know I was there. Nobody did. I really did not leave Oklahoma City after the bus meeting with the firm idea of coming to Diamond Grove. I really didn't. Although it must have been back there in my mind somewhere.

Jess coughed some more and then he waved at me to follow him. He led me around the side of the Diamond Grove City Hall, which was a two-story white concrete building. We turned down an alley and came to an unmarked door that was clearly the rear door to a store or something that faced out on the main street of town on the other side. He took a key from a key chain, unlocked it and went in. I followed.

It was a bank. A vacant, dusty, old bank. There was a row of teller's cages down one side of the narrow building, several desks behind a rail down the other. In the center was a waist-high table for customers to write checks on or to do whatever else they wanted to do. All the furniture was still there. It looked, in fact, like somebody had just locked up for the evening. Except for the dust.

"We can talk in here," Jess said. He pointed toward a desk in the back with a bronze plate on it that said, "President." He walked around behind it and sat down. I took a seat in a chair facing him. Like I was there to see him about a loan on a new Toyota Corolla.

"No wonder you cough all the time," I said. "The dust in here is awful."

"I cough because I am dying," he replied.

"Yes, sir," I said. "But you could still pay somebody to come in here and clean this place up a bit."

"I'd rather spend my money on kids like that out there on that platform, if you don't mind."

I got down to business.

"Jess, we think there's a connection between Sooner Number One and the murders. Nothing else seems to tie them together."

"It's about time somebody got murdered for something that matters," he said. Jess, because of the cough and the handkerchief, seldom locked eyes with the person he was talking to. He appeared to be doing so even less now. I had not got a good straight look from him since I stopped him outside city hall.

"The problem is figuring out the connection and who would have a reason to kill them," I said. "Help me think it through, if you don't mind."

He waved his handkerchief, which was blue, at me.

"Okay, then," I said. "Morgan, Whistle, Little and Freeman suddenly and unexpectedly came out in favor of Sooner Number One. I believe you got 'em to."

He waved his handkerchief.

"Is that a yes or a no?"

"What is wrong with encouraging people to do the right thing? I thought that was part of the democratic process. You petition your government through its officials."

"Not with a suitcase of money."

"We've been through this before." He waved his handkerchief again.

"Why did you come back to Oklahoma, Jess? With all your money you could have gone anywhere, lived anywhere, helped out just about anybody anywhere. Why did you come back here?"

I watched him make a decision. To talk to me or not to talk to me. To have a real conversation with another human being or not to.

"I wanted to have an impact," he said, obviously deciding to talk seriously. For a few moments, at least. "I wanted to know and to see what my money was doing. I wanted to go somewhere and see what a little money could do. I wanted to know the people I gave my money to. I knew that Diamond Grove needed me and my money. I had been away a long time, but I knew it. I knew they needed me and what I had in my suitcase. I knew it."

End of conversation. He stood up and said: "It's time for Tuesday Book and Poetry Club. Come on with me. You can freeload a meal."

Tuesday Book and Poetry Club. It was one of Jess's most publicized innovations in Diamond Grove. The local Rotary, Kiwanis and Lions Club chapters were replaced by weekly luncheons of the Tuesday book thing plus a Wednesday Music Appreciation Society and a Thursday Drama and Theater Society. The Diamond Grove Political Union met on Mondays for debates about current events in Diamond Grove, Oklahoma, America and the world.

We went out the front door to the main street of town, which was called Main Street. The bank was one of several old but deserted buildings on the block. But they all had been spruced up and restored on the outside and appeared ready to be born again. They were another of Jess's projects.

"We're bringing it back," Jess said as we walked along. "Main Street is going to be Main Street again. I've got a real bank going in back there where we were. A department store is going to take over the old department store. There's even a chance of getting a hotel chain to reopen our old hotel. Maybe we could talk that wife of yours into putting in one of her mart things somewhere around here."

"I'm sure she would do it," I said, not really sure of any such thing.

"I heard about her sash," he said. "They tried to give me one of those two years ago, but I told them I had better things to do than accept an award named after a chocolate fork."

The old hotel was where the luncheon was and where we now went in. The lobby was deserted and unused, as were all of the rooms in the place that had once been called the Hotel Diamond, "The Jewel of Southeastern Oklahoma." The only thing open and functioning now was its main ballroom. A restaurant around the corner brought the food in and served it to each of the four weekly luncheons.

Jess shook no hands, made no small talk with his fellow members of the Tuesday Book and Poetry Society. But he did smile and nod and cough pleasantly at them. There were at least four hundred men and women there, milling about, going through the buffet line, finding seats at round tables through-out the ballroom. I followed Jess and got a plate of barbecued ribs, pinto beans, cole slaw and corn bread and a glass of iced tea.

"Napkins," Jess said. "Grab some extras. The ribs, you know."

I took a handful of paper napkins and went with him and our food to a table off to one side. I expected him to sit at the head table, to be treated as the king of this luncheon, as he was of Diamond Grove. I also, frankly, thought it was possible he might even make it known that the lieutenant governor of

Oklahoma was there with him, because of my New York speech if for no other reason.

In introducing me to the dentist, the State Farm agent, the high school English teacher and the tire-store owner at our table he did finally say something: "If you have any complaints about the stupid way our state government operates, here's your chance," he said. "This is the lieutenant governor. The best thing about him is that he's not the idiot who is the governor."

I had never eaten a meal with Jess before. Making a gagging mess of it was something he had in common with C. Harry Hayes. It was fascinating to watch him hold a rib to his mouth for gnawing with his left hand and his blue handkerchief for coughing into between bites with his right. It didn't quite make me sick but it was close.

The program after lunch was about the work of Stephen Dobyns, a writer I had never heard of. The man at the microphone at the head table began by asking everyone if they had read the assigned book, *Saratoga Snapper*. Most of the right hands in the room went up. "And how about Charlie Bradshaw? Isn't he something?" There were noises of agreement. "I like Victor Plotz!" somebody yelled.

I had no idea what was going on, but fortunately the State Farm agent, who was sitting on my right, was a nice and helpful man. He whispered that Dobyns was a writer from somewhere in upstate New York State who wrote detective stories and other kinds of novels. He was also a poet. "He's coming here himself next week to read some of his stuff and talk to us. Updike is next month. He's coming, too. He writes books about a guy named Rabbit. They're really dirty. Jess here pays for it all. We had John Irving last year. And we're trying to get Eudora Welty. We read their stuff and talk about it for three weeks before they come. I want Mickey Spillane to be invited. We vote on them. They spend all day in town. At the elementary and junior and high school, too. Great program. Jess pays for it."

I did not tell him that my wife just got a Chocolate Fork in Chicago with Eudora Welty. But I didn't get a chance to actually meet her.

"Who is Charlie Bradshaw?" I whispered.

"He's the detective this guy Dobyns writes about. Victor Plotz is Charlie's friend. They both get mixed up in some murders."

Maybe C. and I could star in a detective novel about our murders.

I turned away to listen to what the man at the microphone and others in the audience were saying about it all when I got a wave of the blue handkerchief from Jess.

I whispered my good-byes to the State Farm man and the others at our table and followed Jess out of the ballroom to the lobby.

"I haven't read the book, so what's the point?" Jess said. "Good to see you."

"I admire what you do with your money, Jess," I said. "It is simply amazing."

Jess may have been nuts and a murderer, but he loved praise

as much as any sane man who had never killed anybody. He looked directly at me now for the first time. He told me that the drama group was going to read out loud *Death of a Salesman* on Thursday. And that Isaac Stern came to town last year and played all day for everyone in town with the Strings of Diamond Grove. Jess said a deal had just been made for a violinist named Itzhak Perlman to come in January. "He's a twofer," said Jess. "He's a cripple like you. Instead of a missing eye he's on crutches. He'll show the cripples of this town, particularly the little and young ones, that it doesn't have to mean a thing. Not one thing. I love violin music."

He started coughing uncontrollably. It was a deep, wrenching cough.

I wanted to grab him or give him something.

When he finally stopped and removed the handkerchief from his mouth, he said only, "Drive safely."

"You must have some idea about who killed those guys, Jess."

He waved his handkerchief, coughed into it again and said:

"Who killed them doesn't matter. The important thing is that the killers did a good deed for the state of Oklahoma and its people. Let it rest."

"You mean it was a good deed because they had changed their minds about Sooner Number One? They had gone back to the other side, to opposing us?"

No answer.

"How did you know they had changed their minds?"

He gave me a wave of his blue handkerchief and walked

toward the front door of the hotel lobby. He went outside and opened the right-side door of a red International pickup that was parked there at the curb. The skin-headed guy named Jackson was behind the wheel. He now started up the truck and drove it, him and Jess away.

One of the few real special privileges of my office was what I could do with my car. I could park it just about anywhere and I could drive it just about any way I wished without getting ticketed. I seldom took advantage of the privilege because I felt public officials should set an example for lawfulness. What could be a worse message to send to the young people of Oklahoma than for them to see their lieutenant governor parking in yellow loading zones, running red lights or driving east on I-44 at speeds of eighty-five plus miles per hour?

But occasionally exceptions to my lawfulness had to be made.

I had stopped at a JackieMart outside Choctaw for a cold drink and to make a phone call. After getting my drink at the regular drive-through I drove around to another part of the lot where there were three drive-up phones that I could make a call from without getting out of the car. The phone with the

slots and box for dialing and putting in money was on a retract-
able arm. I pulled it over and into the car window, dialed,
talked, hung up and then pushed it back out and drove off. The
drive-up phone was one of the many creations of my brilliant
sash-winning/wearing wife.

The first call was to Janice Alice. She said Sandra Faye
Parsons had called and wondered if there was any answer to
her note? Oh, yes. Her note. I still had it in my coat
pocket somewhere. I would have to get it out and read it. Yes,
indeed.

Janice Alice said C. was desperate to talk to me. So I called
him, but I did not tell him where I was or that I had just been
with Jess Deaton.

"We have a plan to catch Jess and we need you, Mack," he
said.

And away I went up the interstate as fast as my little blue
Buick Skylark would carry me, which was at speeds of eighty-
five plus miles per hour. Any young people of Oklahoma who
saw me speeding would just have to understand it was official
business. It was urgent that I get back to Oklahoma City, to
the seat of government, as fast as possible.

As I pulled out of the JackieMart lot I got a quick glimpse
in my rearview mirror of a man in a green Honda who looked
a lot like Deaton's man Jackson. He had on a blue and white
baseball cap, but there was something in the split second I saw
him that made me think the head underneath the hat was
shaved bald.

It was remotely possible that Jess had had me tailed. A man who could murder four members of the Oklahoma legislature was capable of anything.

■

C. was where he said he would be: at the north end of the empty parking lot behind the National Softball Hall of Fame, which had closed for the day. It was after six o'clock, but there was still daylight. Buck Sporne was with him in the backseat of C.'s Lincoln. When I arrived they both got out and motioned for me to start walking with them. A few glances around here and there made it obvious and clear that there were OBI and FBI agents spread around in trees and other places to make sure that nobody could possibly hear a word the three of us might say.

"Why all of this?" I said after we had walked silently into the empty Hall of Fame's softball stadium. We turned to the right and walked down to seats in the second row up from the right-field dugout.

"You are not going to believe the answer to that question," C. said. He sat down, then Buck sat down and then I sat down between them. The seats were red aluminum. We took those numbered 1,2,3 in the row. Each said "Washington ASA, Kennewick, Washington," on the back, probably meaning that this group had paid for those particular seats.

C., Buck and I sat there together side by side like three

spectators who had showed up to see a ball game on the wrong night. Again, I could see men in dark suits and ties and white shirts around.

"First, some of our guys discovered they were being tailed," C. said. "We even picked up a tail on Buck."

Said Buck: "Fortunately, we were able to double back and follow back and, lo and behold, we think it was Jess Deaton's man, that shaved-head guy Jackson. He was dressed funny, in a wig even, but we are pretty sure it was him."

"When was that?" I asked.

"An hour or so ago," Buck said. "Why?"

"I thought I saw Jackson a while ago down where I was, but clearly that couldn't be. No big deal."

No big deal.

C., again like somebody involved in a two-man presentation at a Lions Club in Purcell or something, nodded toward Buck Sporne of the FBI, son of the Pop Bottle Man.

"I went back to our computer people in Washington," Buck said. "The file on Jess Deaton was clean, maybe too clean. It took some doing, but finally I was told it had been ordered clean by what we call 'Higher Authority—National Security.' So I made some more calls to some of our intelligence people and then some of our former intelligence people and then to some other people I know from some other agencies. Nobody knew much, except it is clear as a pair of glass testicles Jess Deaton at one time did some work for the government of the United States of America. Probably not as an employee but doing some kind of contract work."

Glass testicles?

"What kind of work?" I asked.

"Take your pick, suh. Take your guess."

"But he hasn't gotten to the good part yet," C. said.

Buck continued. "I got a little luckier on this man Jackson. First place his name is not Jackson. It's Adami. John David Adami. He was released from Attica and pardoned in 1965 after serving ten years of a life sentence for murder in the state of New York. He did his killing for a Mafia family. His record is clean as a Johnny Whistle after that, as if he died and went to heaven. The important thing, and the only important thing, is that one file in one office that remained had a name to contact in case of an emergency. Jess Deaton was that name."

I looked out onto the softball diamond. Softball had never been my sport. I always thought there was only one kind of baseball and only one way to play it. With hardballs, big bats, and long distances between bases and to the fences. I knew the Hall of Fame building itself back at the parking lot had photos and memorabilia from the great softball players of all time. But who were they? Who were their Stan Musials, Joe Di-Maggios and Al Pilarciks? Were there softball baseball cards? Were there bats with their signatures engraved on them up there at the top? Had there ever been a softball game on television? Would Vin Scully ever call the play-by-play of a softball game?

"So, what it means, Mack," said my friend C., "is that we have further confirmation—certain confirmation, in my opin-ion—that Jess Deaton is the Capitol Ripper."

"Or, more precisely, that Jess Deaton most likely called the shots and the strangles and the pushes, but John David Adami did the real work," said Buck.

"Precisely," C. said.

Precisely. I needed no further certain confirmation. I knew it was true. Maybe I always knew it.

I looked at each of them and said finally, "It's all so sad and stupid. Jess Deaton was on the right side of things. What he's done down there in Diamond Grove is something to behold. I just came from there. He's got State Farm insurance agents talking about poets who write murder mysteries and things. He's redoing the main street. He's sending kids to college and getting dropouts to drop back in. He's spending his money the way money ought to be spent."

"He's a killer, Mack, ___ it!" C. said. "What do you mean you just came from there?"

"I went by to see him. I was on my way back from Davidson . . . calm down."

"Calm down? Did you talk about murder techniques? The pros and cons of pushing people out of windows compared to strangling them with ribbons? What in the hell were you doing? You could have been killed yourself, for chrissakes!"

"That was not smart, Mr. Lieutenant Governor," said Buck.

"Don't tell me what's smart or what's not smart. I am not the one who made The Cluck my clown!"

"I would remind you, suh, that my clown was not a wanton killer of Oklahoma legislators, as was your clown!"

"Jess Deaton is not my clown!"

"Now, you two calm down, ___ it," C. said.

I gave C. the worst look a one-eyed man could give another man. "Don't you cuss at me, you one-eared Scrambled Dog eater!"

That set Buck off to laughing. "I can't believe what is going on here. We are in the process of solving one of the most convoluted, strange, irritating, embarrassing serial-murder cases in all of history and you two pints of pigeon ___ are going on like two clowns at a Georgia county fair. . . ."

"You can shut up, too!" I said to Buck.

And I stood up and looked across to left field.

Looking at neither of them, I said, "Okay, go arrest him and get it over with."

I took two steps away when C. said, "There's a problem with that, oh Saint Lieutenant Governor One-eyed Mack."

I stopped, turned to face him and said, "What problem?"

"We still can't prove a goddamn cotton-picking thing," he said.

"Not one tiny piece of any of it," Buck added.

"We know what happened, or at least we are sure we know what happened, but they are pros and they have left us not one clue. Nothing."

"You have the tapes, particularly the one with The Cluck and Jess, you have Jackson's killing record," I said. "And Jess knew about Jackie's sash. He told me he did."

"So what?"

"That's where he got the idea for how to do away Johnny

Whistle. Jess would do something like that as a kind of inside joke or something. That's a clue."

"Thank you so much, Mr. Detective Mack," C. said. "The fact is the only way this thing gets solved is with a confession or we catch him in the act."

"You have got to be kidding about confessing," said I. "Jess isn't going to confess. As a matter of simple fact, I just came from kind of trying to get him to confess. I guess that was why I went by there. I was hoping he would tell me what he did. Or maybe I was hoping he would convince me he didn't have anything to do with those killings."

"You could have blown the whole case!" Buck said, his voice rising to a higher pitch than he probably would have preferred.

"But I didn't, did I?" I said. "What have you two law-enforcement geniuses figured out? What is your magic plan that I came speeding back I-44 to hear?"

"Our plan is not to go for a confession anyhow," C. said. "It's to go for trapping him, setting him up to kill again."

"A murder sting?"

"Yeah, you might call it that."

"All we need is a good piece of bait," said Buck.

I turned toward the infield. I played second base in high school. Hardball, of course, not softball. There was something special and wonderful about taking the throw from the short-stop, making the pivot and firing the ball sidearm to first for the double play. I wondered if it was easier for a second baseman in softball. Was there an Eddie Stanky or a Jackie Robinson of softball?

"We set up Jess and his killer man to move on our bait," C. said.

"It's all on videotape, of course," Buck said.

"And carefully controlled, of course, so nobody gets hurt," C. said.

Can you throw a curve with a softball? How in the world could you get the right kind of hold on the ball to make it curve throwing underhanded? I thought of poor Tommy Walt. Those little fingers of his couldn't get a good grip on a hardball. There was no way he could have been a softball pitcher.

"Jess would never buy me as bait," I said to C. and Buck. "I have been on the side of Sooner Number One from the beginning. He'd smell a setup right off if I suddenly decided to go against it. It's a stupid idea. No wonder our country is being overcome with crime and criminals if stopping it is in the hands of folks like you."

"We were thinking of The Chip," C. said.

"Your friend the governor," Buck added.

"Jess already thinks he's an idiot, which he is," C. said. "It would be a natural and a delight for Jess to have him killed in the name of progress for Oklahoma."

"No!" I screamed out to second base and beyond.

■

"Yes!" Joe screamed across his desk and beyond.

That was his reaction only to the news that Jess Deaton was definitely the man responsible for killing The Cluck, Tipp Freeman, Doug Little and Johnny Whistle.

"Yes! Yes! Yes! I told you he was crazy, Mack! I told you Jess Deaton was a menace. We—you—should never have let him back in this state. We should have stopped him at the border, Mack. We need an Oklahoma border patrol. Yes, yes, yes. That is what we need. Oklahoma should be for Oklahomans. Oklahoma for Oklahomans. The Sooner State for Sooner people."

"Jess was born and raised in Oklahoma," I said. "Even if we had a border patrol they would have had to let him through."

It was the next morning. We were in Joe's office. I had had no choice but to go along with C. and Buck Sporne. Jess Deaton may have been a man who wanted only the best for his town and our state, a do-gooder who knew what real good was, a man who had used his money to bring back main streets, to change the lives of many, many people with dropout scholarships, to bring music from people named Stern and Perlman and words from writers named Dobyns, Updike and Welty. But none of that could excuse murder. I was the lieutenant governor of Oklahoma who had sworn to uphold the laws of our state and nation. Clearly and certainly I had to do what I could to bring Jess and his man to justice. I had to do what C. and Buck asked me to do.

I am not proud of how we recruited Joe. But it could have been worse. Buck had argued at first that there was no reason to tell Joe anything. Just set the trap and spring it, he said, using Joe much like a hunter uses a wooden-duck decoy. The hunter doesn't have a heart-to-heart with the decoy, so why should we? I was appalled. There was simply no way we could expose the governor of Oklahoma to being murdered without telling him we were doing it. And getting his permission.

What if he refused to cooperate? Buck had asked.

He won't, C. had replied.

I set up the meeting. Buck tried to get out of coming, but C. and I insisted. Having the FBI involved would help to dramatize the seriousness of the effort and encourage Joe to believe the plan might work.

He stayed behind his desk, with downtown Oklahoma City and Petunia #1, the oil well, outside the window behind him. He put us in three chairs fanned out across from him. I was in the middle, C. on my left, Buck on my right.

We waited out his reaction to the Jess Deaton news and then answered some basic questions about Jess and what Buck had found out about his background.

"You federal people are the source of all that is going wrong in this country," Joe said to Buck. "Here we are, confronted with crimes against the humanity of Oklahoma, and what do we discover? We discover the perpetrator of these heinous crimes once worked for the government of the United States of America. That is where he learned how to kill members of our legislature without leaving so much as a trace. . . ."

"Now, we're not sure he actually worked as an employee," Buck said. "We think it was more as a contract worker . . ."

"Don't tell me what we think! Do not tell me what we think, Mr. Federal Man! You people come down here from Washington and ruin our state. Do not tell me what we think!"

Buck didn't say much after that.

It was I, of course, who began the pitch for Joe's services against the heinous criminal. C. helped here and there, but mostly it was left to me to lay out the proposal for his being bait for murder.

Joe, as always in brown and black in his clothes and in his personality, kept remarkably silent for a while. But then he went directly at me, and only me.

"So, here you sit, Mack, the Second Man of Oklahoma who becomes First Man of Oklahoma if I should ever die before I wake," he said. "Here you sit, recommending to me that I should intentionally become a target of a professional assassin in order to bring him and his accomplice to heel. Here you are, Mack. Here you are in person right here in my office. Here you are, with the director of the Oklahoma Bureau of Investigation, the distinguished Mr. Hayes, and a special agent of the federal government, the Federal Bureau of Investigation, a Mr. Sporne, saying to me, 'Joe, go out and make yourself a target. But be relaxed about it, Joe. We'll protect you. We'll even tape these guys trying to kill you. These killers have already struck four times—but who's counting?—and they have done it perfectly without leaving a tiny clue, without making one tiny mistake. Not one tiny clue, not one tiny mistake, Joe. But relax. They won't bring it off this time because we will be there when they move on you, Joe. We will be there, Joe. We will be there with our agents and our guns and our videotape cameras. Relax, Joe. Relax, Target Joe.' Is that what you're telling me, Mack? Tell me that is what you are telling me, Mack."

"We are convinced Jess Deaton is a killer, Joe," I said for about the tenth time. "The only way we can think of to prove it is to catch him in the act."

"But what if you are slightly slow in the catching, Mack? You got yourself a great piece of videotape that proves, by God, that Jess and his man really are killers. Look at them there killing the governor, old Target Joe. Lookee there! There they are, actually killing old Joe Hayman of Buffalo, the governor! Come one, come all! Popcorn and Milky Ways for all! Come to the videotape watching!

"There's only one problem, Mack. You got your proof and you got yourself the job as governor, but what do I get? I get myself killed. I get myself good and killed. Dead, Mack. I will be dead. Jess and his guy will go to the pen and maybe even to the electric chair at McAlester and that will be really swell for justice, but I won't be around to enjoy it, Mack. I will have preceded them in death, as they say about widows and widowers in the Buffalo, Oklahoma, *Register-Times*. Preceded them in death, Mack. Will you promise to order all Oklahoma flags flown at half-mast for ten or twelve minutes? Will you promise to name something in my memory? How about a turnpike or a state office building? A bridge over the Red River? Will you promise me a Joe Hayman Memorial Overpass, Mack? A Joe Hayman Outdoor Toilet at a roadside park?"

"There are risks in everything, Joe," I said stupidly. "The ones for you in our plan are minimal. I do not know what else to say."

C. suddenly stood up.

"Where are you going, Hayes?" Joe asked. "Where are you going?"

"Out of here is where I'm going," C. said. "Out of here to find some official of this state government besides Mack who believes solving a series of murders is worth doing something about, some official who is not afraid to put a little something on the line, some official who has some faith in the law-enforcement people of this state and nation to do their jobs."

C. started for the door. "Oh, come back and sit down, you blackmailing worm," Joe said. "You've got me and you know it. You knew it from the second you came in here. GOVERNOR REFUSED TO HELP SOLVE RIPPER CASE is a headline I do not need in my life and you know it. Do it or else. Do it or we tell the world you're chicken. Cock-a-doodle-do. Cock-a-doodle-do."

Cock-a-doodle-do.

And we then worked out with him the details of how he would become a decoy for murder.

■

Back at my office, I had a few minutes before I was to take Step One, which would put our plan to catch Jess the Ripper into action.

So I sat down at my desk, the one across from which Johnny Whistle of Enid had recently gone to his reward, and read the note from Sandra Faye.

I smelled it before I read it. I did not and do not know anything about perfumes and fragrances, but I had the feeling I was inhaling something expensive and, well, suggestive. Something with a name that probably suggested something more than a professional relationship about mummies and other matters historical.

I hated myself for thinking such a thing. I really did.

Her note was handwritten. It said:

My dear Mack,

Here I am again on my knees in front of you, figuratively speaking, of course. Here I am again begging you to help, begging you to come to our rescue.

We are at a crisis stage with the mummies, Mack. I have been unable to raise any money at all either through state

and official sources or through foundations and private do-
nors. No one or institution has thus far seen the emergency
and thus the vision. I have thus far kept the press out of the
basement but I cannot do so much longer. A string of embarrassing stories and photographs of and about those mummies looms in our future if something is not done.

I would welcome the opportunity to personally show you
and demonstrate the nature of the emergency. Do you have
any plans to come to Enid anytime soon? If not, could you
make a special trip? The intensity of the emergency warrants
such a trip.

We—you and I—have created something that is bigger
than both of us. We must not turn our backs on it or each
other now.

> With deepest respect and affection,
> Sandra Faye.

I folded the note back up, returned it to its envelope and
stuck it in the middle drawer of my desk.

The official business of Johnny Whistle's funeral would in
fact be taking me to Enid very soon.

■

I took Step One in the plan to snare Jess at three o'clock. Using
my office phone, which had been outfitted with a recorder, I

got Jess Deaton on the line. He was at his warehouse office in Oklahoma City.

"Jess, I've got some bad news," I said.

"Who's dead now?" he asked.

"Nobody. It's Joe Hayman."

"He's brain-dead."

"He's changed his mind about Sooner Number One."

"Why?"

"Don't know for sure," I said. "But he says he'll veto it if it does pass the legislature."

"The man's a one hundred percent pure-bred nincompoop," Jess said.

"Are you interested in talking to him?"

"You suggesting I bribe the governor of Oklahoma? Is that what you, the one, the only Mr. Clean One-eyed Mack, are suggesting? I am shocked and I am stunned."

"Shut up, you old fool," I said, wondering how Buck and C. were going to take to my approach when they listened to the tape later. "I'm just trying to tell you we've got a problem."

"I'll take care of it," Jess said.

"How?"

"Trust me."

"I don't want any bribing, Jess."

"Maybe I'll tip off the Ripper so he can do away with him," Jess said.

"That's not funny, Jess. Look, while I have you on the line, I may need a grant of money to solve the mummy problem up in Enid. Are you interested in coming to the aid of a woman in distress?"

"I thought the mummy was a man. John Wilkes George or something. The whole thing sounds idiotic. How much do you need?"

"I don't know for sure. We haven't really priced it out yet. . . ."

"I'm not sure I'm interested in using my money to solve mummy crises, Mister Lieutenant Governor. I have more important things to do with it and to do now." And he hung up on me.

I did not care what Buck and C. might think about my making the mummy pitch. I am not proud of what I did, but it had to be done.

It was also good cover, as they say in law enforcement.

■

Jess wasted no time. He and Jackson were at Joe's office first thing the next morning. They just showed up there at the capitol and demanded to see the governor. Joe dropped everything, of course, and had Jess come in. Jackson remained in the small waiting room outside the governor's office. The woman behind the desk looked and acted like she was a regular secretary-type receptionist. But she was actually a heavily armed female agent of the Oklahoma Bureau of Investigation.

It was also an electronically monitored entrance. A metal detector had been installed around the door to the outer office. It seemed unlikely that Jess and Jackson would show up with a gun and start shooting, but C. and Buck decided to take no chances on anything. They could not take a chance on Jess's really killing Joe. Agents in cars and on foot also followed Jess and Jackson every step and breath of the way they took to the capitol, as they would until the trap sprung.

Assuming it did.

Jess was in Joe's office for less than twenty minutes. C., Buck and I watched and listened to the whole thing from an anteroom next door in which Buck had assembled an electronic video and recording system like the one he used in his Operation Sooner Broken Trust sting.

In grainy black-and-white pictures with tinny sound we heard Joe say, "Most people call ahead before they come see the governor of Oklahoma."

"I'm not most people, am I? I'm here to tell you there's a rat in your nest," Jess said. He grabbed a dark-colored handkerchief out of his pocket and coughed. And coughed. "Mack is out to get your ___. He just told me you had turned on the education thing. It's a lie, isn't it? Why would Mack do something like that? Maybe having one eye makes you crazy. That Hayes is nuts, too. Maybe it's because he has only one ear. Do you have only one of something you should have two of, Joe?

It wouldn't surprise me because you are nuttier than both of them and then some."

He coughed again.

Joe said, "Don't you ever come in here or anywhere else even suggesting that somebody else is crazy. My God almighty, they have red brick buildings all over this country stuffed full of people like you in padded cells slobbering all over themselves. In a padded cell, Jess Deaton. That is where you belong. Padded with big pads. Lots and lots of big pads. Locked up and away with those pads for the rest of your natural life. Assuming your life is natural, which I do not assume. Now, what is it you want to know? Ask your question and get out of here so I can continue doing what the people of this state elected me to do. And that, I can assure you, was not dealing with loony lugs like you even if you are rich. Yeah, I know you're rich. Rich, rich, rich. Big deal, Jess. Big deal. Now, what is it?"

"What's it going to take to bring you back to your senses on Sooner Number One?"

"Up to your bribing, is that it? Got that suitcase full of money for the governor, is that it? Is that it, Jess? Well, take your suitcase and shove it up your padded cell, Jess. Shove it so far up that padded cell of yours that it'll look like confetti instead of dollars. I have business to attend to. Get out of here and get out of here now. I have to go dedicate the first use of restaurant grease in the gas tank of an intercity bus. I have multiple funerals to attend. I have many other important matters like that to see to. I am an important person, Jess, and you ain't. Now, get out of here."

"Aren't you afraid the Ripper'll get you?" Jess said as he coughed and stood.

"The Ripper's obviously some demented fool with the guts of old restaurant grease," Joe said. "When I start letting that kind of thing scare me is when I start looking around for some line of work other than being the leader of the Sooner men, women and children of Oklahoma."

"You are not any more the leader of the men, women and children of this state than Piggly Wiggly is."

"Who in the ___ is Piggly Wiggly?"

"He's an old man in Waurika who started a grocery store chain in the thirties."

"Get out of here, Jess. I don't need your money, I don't need your threats, I don't need your stupid stories. Nobody in history was ever named Piggly Wiggly. And even if there was, he wasn't from Waurika. Nobody's from Waurika. Nobody's from Waurika, Jess. And nobody's from Diamond Grove either. Nobody."

"You fool," Jess said as he walked out. The hidden microphone barely caught his last words, which were, "Sic 'em, Ripper."

"Don't threaten me!" Joe screamed after him. "Don't threaten me." Then he said in a quiet voice, "Hey, you forgot your peanuts."

Jess was long gone and did not hear it. But C. and Buck sure did. C. lunged for a phone and called for the OCPD bomb squad. Buck raced into Joe's office. I went with him.

Joe was still standing there with a bag of peanuts in his right hand.

"Deaton brought these things in here?" Buck asked.

"Right. Right," Joe said. "He went off and forgot 'em. Right."

Buck grabbed the bag out of Joe's hand and ran from the office.

■

The peanuts turned out to be just peanuts. No bombs, poisons or other deadly things were in them. They were even saltless. The OBI lab people called C. with the word.

A few minutes later Joe and I walked out of the governor's office the regular public way around to the west-side second-floor elevator. As usual when Joe traveled, an armed highway patrolman in a regular dark blue suit and red tie was with us. FBI and OBI people in work clothes and tourist clothes hovered about acting like they weren't FBI and OBI people.

We rode down to the crummy first floor of the building and out the even crummier entrance to the west parking lot where we officials parked our cars. The governor's official dark blue Chrysler sedan was waiting for us just outside the door with the motor running. So were several FBI and OBI people dressed as gardeners and parking-lot sweepers.

I climbed in back with Joe, the highway patrolman jumped into the right-side front seat and the driver, also a plainclothes patrolman, drove us off to our known encounter with a post-oil society and to a possible unknown one with a gubernatorial assassin.

"So, how am I doing?" Joe asked. "How am I doing, Mack?"

"Great, Joe," I replied. "Great, Joe." Joe repeated himself a lot and I tended to do the same thing after being with him a while. "The show you put on for Jess was absolutely incredible. Absolutely incredible."

"If I get killed, that'll be a show I'll never forgive you for," he said. "I will haunt you, Mack. I mean really haunt you. You may be the governor and they'll make a big deal about your being the first one-eyed one in history and all of that, but you will never be happy. Never, Mack. Everywhere you look, everywhere you step, there I will be. In ghost form. In ghost form, Mack. Joe Hayman of Buffalo will not only not go quietly, he will not go at all. At least not from your mind and soul. Always, Mack. I will be there to remind you of what you did. Always, Mack."

"Nothing's going to happen to you, Joe," I said. "Nothing's going to happen to you."

"I want the tape of what I just did released if it does, Mack. I want every television station in Oklahoma to broadcast me standing up to Jess Deaton. Pass a law and sign it making them do it if they won't on their own, Mack. Promise me you will do that. Promise. I want that tape seen by everybody. Promise me, Mack."

"I hereby promise you, Joe."

"Will you promise one more thing, Mack? Just one more thing?"

"Certainly, Joe. Anything."

"Have me mummified. Have me mummified and put under glass maybe there in the rotunda of the capitol until the end of Oklahoma time. Could you do that, Mack? Can you promise me you will turn me into a mummy?"

"I can so promise, Joe. I can so promise."

We had arrived at the office and shops of the Oklahoma Blue Arrow Motorcoaches.

■

A little crowd of fifty or so people was gathered in the parking lot right behind a 1972 GMC bus. A microphone was set up there. A couple of TV cameras on tripods were also off to the side, along with reporter-looking people with still cameras and notebooks.

Joe jumped out of the car like he had never been happier to be anyplace in his life. He shook every hand thrown his way, even those that belonged to the various detectives and agents who clearly made up at least half of the audience. Maybe two thirds.

One of C.'s men, as prearranged, came directly to me and whispered the prearranged word: "Green." That meant that neither Jess nor Jackson was anywhere to be seen. I walked casually over to Joe and whispered the same word to him.

Bill Hylton of Oklahoma Blue Arrow went to the microphone and started the festivities.

"This marks an historic day for us at Oklahoma Blue Arrow and maybe for Oklahoma and the world," he said. "Today, with the help of our governor, we will begin an experiment that could lead to a new order in the world of energy, the main kind of energy to us in the bus business, the kind we put in our gas tanks."

He introduced the two professors and he introduced Tommy Walt, calling him "not only the son of our lieutenant governor and one of our region's leading collectors of old restaurant grease but also a former employee of ours here at Oklahoma Blue Arrow."

Then he invited Joe to join him at the microphone and handed him a ten-gallon can painted in alternating one-inch-high red, white and blue stripes. "In this can," said Bill, "is a magic mixture of methanol and some grease Tommy Walt's people collected just last night from the McDonald's on Northwest Sixty-third Street. If you, sir, would please pour it in the gas tank of this bus."

Joe did as he was told, carrying the can around to the right rear of the blue and white bus. A cone-shaped siphon was in place. Joe tipped the can just right and poured the magic mixture into the tank. He then handed the empty can to Bill and returned to the microphone.

"It is with pleasure that I do the pouring this morning," he said. "As Neil Armstrong said, you have to start somewhere. One small step for man could be one huge step for mankind. One really huge step for mankind. And that is how I see this pouring this morning. One small pouring of this mixture into this gas tank could be one huge pouring for mankind."

He turned to a uniformed Oklahoma Blue Arrow driver who was standing off to the side. "Driver, start the engine."

The driver, a man in his forties in fully pressed and starched gray, saluted his governor and walked briskly to the front of the bus. We watched as he closed the door.

There was a whirring of the starter and then the motor caught. Quickly, perfectly, wonderfully. The bus drove off in a small cloud as Joe and I and the rest of the people in the crowd applauded and the TV cameras recorded the event for the nightly news. And for history.

"Oh, smell those exhaust fumes," Joe said into the microphone. "Pure hamburger heaven. Pure hamburger heaven."

In a few minutes Joe and I were back in the car on the way to the downtown executive airport.

"How in the ___ I ever let you talk me into pouring old hamburger grease into the gas tank of a bus in public is more than I will ever understand," Joe said to me. "How in the ___ did it happen, Mack? How, Mack? I kept thinking what the stories would say if crazy Jess did strike while I was pouring.

They'd say, Well, old Joe Hayman deserved to die. Anybody crazy enough to pour old hamburger grease into a bus in public deserved to die. Like a mad dog with rabies. Put him out of his misery. Kill him. Kill him.

"He's all yours, Ripper. Sic 'em, sic 'em, Ripper. Sic 'em."

We flew away in the state's Cessna 270, a seven-seater, two-engine plane. Joe looked out the window after takeoff and then across the aisle to me and said, "Jess could afford to buy a missile, Mack. A missile. He's probably down there aiming one at us right now. In a minute, there's going to be a boom and then there's going to be the end. The end, Mack. The end of Target Joe and the One-eyed Mack. We'll probably not feel a thing. Not a thing, Mack. There goes the mummification, too. There would be nothing to mummify, Mack. If it happens, promise me you will keep that tape of my pouring old grease down the tank of that bus off of television. Make it against the law to run if you have to. I want your word, Mack. I want your promise."

"You have it, Joe."

I elected not to remind him that if the plane did go boom in a minute or two, it would mean that I would die, too. Meaning . . . well, that I would not be replacing him as First Man of

Oklahoma and thus would not be in a position to keep anything off or on television. But I said nothing. I chose instead to look in silence out my window as the plane swung around toward the northwest for the twenty-minute flight to Enid, stop one on our day of funerals.

Sandra Faye Parsons knew I was coming. I had Janice Alice call and make arrangements to go to the basement. I had to. I could no longer avoid doing so. I could no longer avoid confronting the problem of the mummies. And that meant confronting Sandra Faye, the woman Jackie called "my girlfriend," which was not so.

Not so at all.

"Green," said the highway patrolman who met us at the plane at the Enid airport. He took us in a patrol car led and followed by local police cars directly to the Northside Baptist Church for the funeral of Johnny Whistle.

It was an open-casket event. Joe and I were there in the front row during the entire service staring at a side view of Johnny Whistle, who was made up like a girl, dressed up like a banker, but otherwise looked pretty much the way he did when I found him with the OU sash around his neck.

"Johnny would have been proud and honored to have both the governor and the lieutenant governor of our state, his state, here this morning," said the preacher from the pulpit. "He would have been happy to know that they and all of Oklahoma mourn his untimely and awful death at the hands of a cowardly, sinful killer of man and soul for whom God will show no mercy when he is apprehended. But we are not here this afternoon to speak of dastardly killers. We are here to speak of the place in heaven God has taken our friend, loved one and public servant, Johnny Whistle. We mourn for his departure, but we should rejoice in his arrival. For he has left this place we call Oklahoma for a better place, the only place better than Oklahoma, a place God and we call Heaven, and eventually, as in the case of Johnny Whistle, call home."

The preacher was a too-thin, too-tanned guy in his early forties in a light blue suit with a Johnny Cash voice, string tie, long black hair over his ears, wire-rimmed aviator glasses, a white leather–covered Bible in his right hand, big gold rings on the fingers of his left hand and stupid words about death and God in his mouth.

"Thank God Jess didn't murder you in that church," I said to Joe when we were back in the car. "I can't imagine anything worse than having that phony praying over your body. Where do they get those guys, Joe? How in the world could anybody in their right mind follow him to a Piggly Wiggly much less to glory? How in the world, Joe? How in the world?"

Joe nodded in agreement. He was clearly stunned at my outspokenness. So was I.

We had an hour before we took off for Ponca City and our second funeral. He was going to drop me at the Museum of the Cherokee Strip while he made the rounds at the *Enid News*, the courthouse and a few lawyers' offices.

"Is there any way, do you think, Joe, that we could come up

with some special money for this museum to solve the mystery of the mysterious mummies?" I asked as we turned down Fourth Street to the museum.

"I am going to do you a favor, Mack," Joe said. "I am going to sit here on this backseat of this car and continue to let my mind concentrate on the fiscal, mass-murder and other problems of our state and pretend that I never heard what you just said. I did not hear you say something so incredibly irresponsible as to suggest that the state of Oklahoma pay out hard-earned taxpayers' money to solve a problem you created by deviating from my speech on national television. I did not hear you say a thing, Mack. Not one thing. My mind is on whether I am going to be killed, on roads and bridges, textbooks and teachers' salaries, on drugs and gang wars, libraries for the young and prisons for the wicked, suitable electric chairs for Jess Deaton and his henchman. I do not want to be embarrassed by those mummies, Mack, and I do not want to be involved in the solution. That is a problem created by you and that woman Parsons; it is one for you and that woman Parsons to solve. I understand she's a looker. Is that right, Mack?"

I shrugged and said nothing. We were at the museum.

■

I am not even going to try to describe Sandra Faye Parsons. Other than to say she was in her late thirties, her hair was white-blond, her complexion resembled vanilla ice cream and she filled out her clothes rather well and snugly. Did she qualify for the label "looker"? It would probably depend on who was doing the looking. The important thing was that she was the director of the Oklahoma Historical Society's Museum of the Cherokee Strip and that she had several advanced degrees in Oklahoma and other kinds of history and was considered one of our state's top historians.

And there were her eyes, which were dark brown and came on beacon-bright when she greeted me at the museum door.

"Oh, thank the Lord you are here," she said, taking my right hand in both of hers. "Once again, it's the One-eyed Mack to the rescue. The dear, sweet, one-and-only One-eyed Mack."

"Please, let's not speak too soon about rescuing. I read your note, received your message, but that does not mean I have a solution. I have nothing in the works . . ."

She turned and pulled me behind her toward an unmarked door to the left just inside the front lobby.

"You are going to be knocked out by what we have in our basement, Mack. You are really going to be knocked out."

She had that right.

First, there was the smell. On the wooden steps going down I picked it up. Was it the odor of formaldehyde? Dill-pickle juice? Gasoline? Vinegar? All of them mixed together?

So this is what mummies smell like.

And there they were. Twelve of them. An even dozen mummies, sitting in chairs, leaning against the walls, lying on tables around the room, which looked to be the standard cement-wall basement found in a standard three-bedroom house. In a quick glance around I saw two women, two young men who looked more like animals than people, in addition to a few middle-aged or elderly men.

"Allow me to introduce you to our little family, Mack. Our family of mummies."

She took me to a mummy woman of forty-five or so dressed in an Indian squawlike costume. "This is the latest one. It was sent anonymously by somebody in Canada."

"Anonymously?"

"Several came in that way. No return address, just turned up in a box or a crate at our door. One was in an orange plastic trash bag."

"I don't get it," I said.

"Guilt."

"Guilt?"

"You know those free days they have at libraries when you can return all overdue books and not pay a fine? Well, these are people turning in mummies they should not have had. As a practical matter, probably no private citizen should have ownership or possession of a mummy. They all belong in museums."

I still did not get it.

"But I specifically said in my speech that we were looking for the mummy of an old man," I said, looking across the wall at a woman sitting in a rocker. She was dressed in a fireman's outfit. "Isn't that another woman over there?"

"Yes. She came identified as the first woman fire chief in

Alabama, but the return address on the UPS package was someplace in Missouri. Trenton, Missouri, I think. There is also a gorilla, and a human cow."

Sandra Faye pointed toward a mummy standing over in a corner. It had the body of a man in a dark blue suit but the head of a dark brown cow.

"And there are four kids." She motioned toward another corner, where there was a boy in an old-fashioned baseball uniform holding a bat, a girl in a swimsuit, a boy in knickers and a girl in a pink and white thing that resembled a pinafore.

"None of this makes any sense," I said. "I had no idea . . . well, I had no idea there were this many mummies out there."

"Nobody did, Mack. It has been one of the great secrets of our time that your actions, your words, finally brought out into the open."

That seemed a little extreme to me. How can something be a secret if nobody cares whether it's told or not? Why should anybody care about knowing there are many mummies out there?

We walked together around the room, stopping a few seconds at each mummy. Conditions varied greatly. Some looked in the best of condition, but most had problems. Pocked or scratched skin, hair that was falling out, mashed noses, missing ears, arms and legs.

There was even one man in a distinguished business suit who had only one eye.

"The least you could do is put an eye patch on this guy," I said.

"I thought about it," said Sandra Faye, "but, frankly, I thought you might take offense if and when people started making the connection between it—him—and you."

The connection between it—him—and you.

For those who either missed or forgot it, the time has come to tell the mummy story. I will try to make it as brief as possible.

I delivered the keynote address at the last Democratic National Convention. I did so as a substitute for Buffalo Joe, who collapsed there in a back room at Madison Square Garden in New York City minutes before he was to go on. One of the veins in his head experienced a temporary blockage of some kind. It was to have been Joe's few minutes in the national sun that might have even led to his being on the national ticket. Every moment and possibility became mine instead.

I had spent hours helping Joe rehearse his speech, so when he asked that I deliver it for him I agreed. I did so almost word for word until the very end, when I got carried away and said the following to the Democrats in Madison Square Garden and to another eighty million Americans of all kinds watching on television:

"We in Oklahoma have our own special search under way for something very special to our history, to our heritage. It is for the remains of a person. A person who died in Enid, Oklahoma, in January 1903. He died of his own hand. He died with the story of a presidential assassination on his lips. His name was

David E. George, but he said to some that he was in fact John Wilkes Booth and that another man had died and been buried in his place. Was he telling the truth? Was he the real John Wilkes Booth? We do not know, because the body of David E. George, perfectly preserved by an Enid mortician as were mummies in olden times, has disappeared. But we know deep down in our Oklahoma souls that it is still out there somewhere. If someone—anyone in hearing distance of my voice—knows where that body is, please let us know. Please contact the Oklahoma Historical Society. Please help us return a little bit of us to its proper home. Someone out there has in their home, their basement, their attic, their office, a mummy that rightfully belongs in Enid, Oklahoma. Would you please help us find that person and help us return it to Enid? Please?"

The convention delegates and spectators went wild and so did a lot of others, including David Brinkley on television. He suggested that I go on the shortlist for vice-president because "the country could do with a national candidate with a search for a mummy as a priority." Senator Daniel Michael Griffin of New Jersey, the Democratic presidential nominee, took David Brinkley's suggestion, but I didn't last long on the shortlist. I came back to Oklahoma earth a few days later still what I was, am and will always be proud to be—the lieutenant governor of Oklahoma.

It was Sandra Faye who had told me about the mummy of David E. George. She was the one who put the story in my head in such a way that it simply popped out like that at the end of my speech.

Now she and I were in the basement of her museum forced to deal with the consequences. The American people had responded to my call. They had sent us their mummies.

"Are any of these mummies David E. George, is the question," I said. It certainly was the question.

"Not that we know of, is the answer," Sandra Faye said. "But there is simply no way to tell for sure."

"You have a photograph of the guy. Check each for the resemblance." The photograph was a black-and-white eight-by-ten that had hung in the museum for years. There was a clipping of an old story in the *Enid News* with it and it was her reading of that clipping that got Sandra Faye interested in launching a search for the mummy of David E. George. The story said the mummy had disappeared from the attic of a rooming house in Philadelphia in the 1950s after ending its career as a third-rate attraction in a variety of third-rate carnivals and other small-time traveling shows.

Sandra Faye, now in the basement, was wearing a blue knit dress that seemed to highlight the movement of her body more than some other kind might have. I could not help but watch the movement as she went over and picked up the eight-by-ten black-and-white photograph of George from a table.

She said: "Here, you take this and go through them and see if you can tell. Just look at the men, if you want. Do it, Mack, and you will see our problem."

I did it and I saw her problem. The photo was old and was of the full David E. George mummy sitting in a chair with a newspaper in his lap. It was the same one she had showed me the day I came by before the Democratic convention, when she planted the whole idea in my head. The facial features were not precise.

At least four of the mummies resembled the photo in some way or another. But they, too, were imprecise in the faces. Age was also hard to determine, except for the kids, because of the aging of the mummies themselves.

"So, what do you do?" I asked, putting a slight emphasis on the word *you.*

"I am afraid, Mack, there is only one thing for us to do," she replied, putting a slight emphasis on the word *us.* "As I have said to you before, we are going to have to spend some money on some experts on mummies. There is no other way."

"How much money?"

She returned to the small table in the center of the room and returned with a small stack of papers. "Here are the bids," she said. "The cheapest is fifty-six thousand dollars, the highest is one hundred eleven thousand six hundred dollars. There are two in between."

"There are four companies in America who are in the business of identifying mummies?" I asked, thinking that Jackie would be delighted to learn that there are even stranger ways to make a living than collecting old restaurant grease.

Although she would not be delighted to learn that I got that information from Sandra Faye Parsons. I had made a terrible mistake after the New York speech in identifying Sandra Faye to Jackie. For reasons I cannot explain, I told Jackie that Sandra Faye, the woman at the Enid museum who had started the whole mummy thing, was "in her sixties." It wasn't long afterward that a photo of Sandra Faye in the *Daily Oklahoman* showed her to be nothing of the kind. Jackie never asked about it or confronted me directly, but it was right afterward that she started referring to Sandra Faye as my girlfriend.

She was not my girlfriend.

"They are not companies," Sandra Faye said. "They are laboratories at museums and universities that do research on mummies."

"What kind of work do they do for their money?"

"We get full analysis of all twelve mummies as to their origin, ages and so on plus a best-shot attempt at identifying all twelve by name. Nobody will guarantee IDs. But they will take fingerprints and things like that and hope for the best. Most of them believe they could get the FBI to cooperate on the fingerprint checks. They have a large computer of some kind in Washington full of millions of fingerprints."

I looked around the basement again at her family of mummies. "Why not simply declare one of these guys David E. George and be done with it?" I said. "Who would ever know the difference?"

"Mack! That would be a lie, a lie to the people and to the history of Oklahoma! I cannot believe you of all people would suggest such a thing!"

I couldn't believe it either. I was not proud of either the thought or the fact that I had said it. There was that fine line again.

"Why not just check out the four or five who look most like David E. George, then?" I said.

"No! Mack! How can we ignore all of the others? Don't they deserve to be treated as . . . well, as real people, too?"

I told her I would do what I could to raise some money, but thus far I had had no luck.

"Please hurry, Mack. There are serious storage problems."

"The smell is terrific, yes," I said, heading for the stairs. "What exactly is that odor?"

"It's more than one, Mack. Each mummy has its own distinctive odor. Each must be seen as an individual person, which is exactly what they are."

I repeated my pledge to do what I could to raise some money.

She walked slowly, ever so slowly, over to me. She put her hands, both of them, up on my face around the cheeks.

"You are truly a special person, Mr. One-eyed Mack. If it were not inappropriate for a state employee to embrace the lieutenant governor, I would do so right here in front of these twelve mummies . . . and let the chips fall where they may."

I would have preferred she had not used the chips analogy, but it was a small point. The fact of the matter was that I wanted very much for her to embrace me. I wanted very much to do at that moment what I had never done since I married Jackie, which was to have a physically intimate relationship with another woman. This woman, Sandra Faye Parsons.

Fortunately, she *was* a state employee and the scene and the smell and the company of twelve mummies were not conducive to a physically intimate relationship.

Fine lines were turning up everywhere in my life.

I decided then and there that no matter what happened with the mummies, I would make absolutely sure that I never ever again found myself in this situation. I would never ever again allow myself to be alone with Sandra Faye Parsons in a basement or any similar place.

With or without mummies.

■

Buffalo Joe gave me a wink when I got back into the car with him for the trip back to the Enid airport.

"You're not ___ that Parsons woman, are you, Mack?" he asked.

"No!"

"That's good, Mack. That is good. Because more men of government and politics and public service have been felled by falling trousers than all of the assassins, plane crashes, felonies, misdemeanors, frauds, revolutions and votes combined and then doubled twice."

I already knew that but I said nothing.

"Remember that, Mack. Remember it as you contemplate doing something irregular, most particularly with an employee of the state of Oklahoma. Doing it with an employee of the state of Oklahoma is a triple-play disaster. The ball goes from first to second to home, which is where they send you when it's over. You like baseball, you get the picture, you understand the play. First to second to home. Remember that."

I said I would.

"It's a historical fact I am talking about, Mack. Fact as in truth and consequences."

I nodded and smiled and shook my head, the face on which had turned warm and a very bright OU red.

■

The next preacher was a Methodist who conducted the most unusual funeral service I had ever attended. It was for State Representative Willard (Tipp) Freeman, the one who had gone out a window of the Park Plaza. The funeral was in Ponca City, where another highway patrolman gave us a "Green" after a twenty-five-minute flight east from Enid.

What remained of Freeman was very little and was not on display. He had been cremated, an unusual way to go in Oklahoma, where open caskets and full burials and graveside services were the preferred and most accepted way to go. I wondered what caused cremation to happen to Freeman, but there was nobody to ask except his family and that would have been improper.

Hey, there, Mrs. Freeman, cremating bodies is what they do

up north, not here in Oklahoma. Why did you do it to your son, Mrs. Freeman?

The service was not in a church or a mortuary but in the ballroom of a mansion that had been built by an eccentric oil millionaire and politician in the 1920s. His name was E. W. Marland, one of the founders of what is now the Continental Oil Company—Conoco. There was some of Jess Deaton in Marland, or the other way around. He did not kill members of the legislature, but he did give away millions of his dollars to churches, schools and to the people and city of Ponca City. He gave away so much, in fact, that it contributed to his dying in 1941 at the age of sixty-seven with very little of it left. What he left behind was not only a beautifully landscaped and built little city of twenty-seven thousand but also a corporate legacy of health, education and other employee benefits. Like Jess, Marland believed in using his money for things that mattered. But unlike Jess, he also believed in using some of it for his own pleasure. The three-story mansion had fifty-five rooms, twelve of which were bathrooms, and was patterned after one in Italy. Florence, Italy. The place also had three kitchens, a leather-lined elevator, a handball court, a huge T-shaped swimming pool, five lakes, a nine-hole golf course, polo grounds, stables and just about everything else a person would need to have the ultimate life of luxury. They called it the Palace on the Prairie, and that was exactly what it was. Now it was owned by the city of Ponca City, which opened it to tourists and rented it out for special occasions. Like memorial services for fallen members of the Oklahoma legislature.

Joe and I again were given front-row seats. There were two hundred or so folding chairs set up in the ballroom, a huge room with a gold-leaf ceiling and crystal chandeliers. Marland, who was the tenth governor of Oklahoma, had had one of his inaugural balls there. Now it was a funeral parlor this day.

Sitting in Marland's mansion at a funeral for a man killed by a man who was a lot like Marland struck me as a most unusual coincidence of history.

"Tipp would be appalled by all of this fuss we are making about him," said the preacher, a well-dressed, normal-looking man in his early fifties. He stood behind a small lectern on a small platform down in front of all of us. "As most of you know, I was his cousin. He felt fuss, particularly about matters of the soul and religion, should be done in private. We argued many a night long into the night about what God meant to him and to me and to you and to all men and women. We argued about the meaning of life itself and of why we are here and what we are supposed to do while we are here. Nobody ever won those arguments. It was not intended that anyone win them.

"We talked about death. On one of those long nights we even talked about this afternoon. Not this specific afternoon but about an afternoon, if he preceded me in death, where I would speak at a service marking his death. Death. Yes, I said *death*. Tipp insisted that night that I never ever use any phony euphemisms. *Death* is the word. Use it, Cousin, he said. Using it, I am.

"He had one other request. And only one other. He asked

that I do for him in death what he lacked the courage to do in life. He asked me to take him out of the closet. Tipp was a homosexual. He was not ashamed of it, but he wanted a career in politics and the two did not mix. Not now, not yet, in Oklahoma. He asked me to explain to you and to all others who will hear of my words and react to them that homosexuality was not a choice he made. It was one God made for him. He said to say that he realized many do not believe that in the abstract and will not believe that in the specific concerning him. But that, he said to say on this afternoon, was the truth. His truth. Take or leave it, believe it or not. That is that. Let us pray."

It was only in that moment that I moved my only eye, the right one, to see what I might see on the faces of the people around me. All I could see was horror. I have never been in a more silent place. Never.

"Dear God in Heaven, take care of Willard Tipp Freeman. Take good care of him. He was a loving human being, a man who cared about people and ideas, a man who laughed and cried, a man who deserved to live a longer and fuller life, a man who will be missed by those of us who knew and loved him. He asked that I ask you, God, on this occasion on his behalf that you help his family, friends and acquaintances understand and appreciate what he asked me to do this afternoon and why it had to be done. In your name, as always, we pray. Amen."

Joe said, "Amen." I said, "Amen." But I heard no others. Somebody at a grand piano off in a rear corner of the ballroom started to play a song. It was a classical piece I did not recognize.

Joe had not looked at me and he did not now as we turned, each in our way, to shake hands with the silent, stunned people around us. I had no idea who they were. I went over to the preacher.

"I am the lieutenant governor," I said, extending my right hand. "That was not an easy thing you just did, sir."

"Thank you for realizing that," he said. "Many are going to wonder why I did not keep his secret. But the choice was not mine."

"I understand," I said. But I was not sure I meant it. I was not sure of anything. Except that I now knew what it was instead of money that had turned and returned Tipp Freeman on the issue of Sooner Number One.

Joe and I were ushered quickly and efficiently back to the car, which took a back way out of the mansion grounds by the guest house. It was there that Marland died in 1941 because that was where he and his wife had been forced to move to because they were too broke by then to maintain their lifestyle in his palace. That wife at the end was his second one, by the way. She was twenty years younger than him and had originally been his adopted daughter. He had to get the adoption annulled so that he could marry her.

Everyone has their fine lines.

"Jess can do me in now," Joe said as the car turned up the road leading back to the airport. "I have now seen and heard everything. Everything, Mack. I have now seen and heard it all. Can you believe what we saw and heard on this day? In the possible sights of a crazy assassin while doing it? In the sights of an assassin with cops saying 'Green' all of the time and it's all happening. All of this. Can you believe any of all of this, Mack? Any of it? Can you, Mack? Can you? Is this politics? Is it government? What is it, Mack?"

"I don't know, Joe," I replied. "I don't know."

And he hadn't even been with me to see the mummies and Sandra Faye Parsons.

■

"Green," said the agent who opened the Cessna's door back at the Oklahoma City airport, the small one just over the Canadian River south of downtown that was used only for small executive aircraft.

C. and Buck were waiting for us in a small hangar some twenty yards away.

"There was no sign of any overt moves of any kind toward you," C. said to Joe. "We had Deaton and his man under tight, unbroken physical and electronic surveillance all day. Both of them hung out at the warehouse in the morning, they had lunch together at a pizza place on May Avenue and then drove back to Diamond Grove late this afternoon. As of a few minutes ago both were safely attending a concert by the Strings of Diamond Grove."

"What does it mean?" Joe said. "What are you telling me?"

"I am telling you what I just told you," C. replied. "Which is that there were no signs of anything today."

"Does it mean you were wrong? Does it mean they were not the killers of the others? Does it mean they've retired from murder? Does it mean our little trick didn't trick? Does it mean my life is no longer at risk? Does it mean I sleep well tonight? Tell me, Mister Director, what are you really telling me?"

Before C. could answer, which was probably just as well, there came the sound of an explosion from outside the hangar. It shook and rattled the tin hangar.

We all ran to the door. The state's Cessna 270, the one the First Man and the Second Man of Oklahoma had just climbed out of, was engulfed in flames that were hot and high.

"I think we need another plan, suh," Buck said to C.

"Precisely," C. replied.

"What was the name of the music Jess and Jackson were safely listening to?" Joe shouted. "Was it Bach or the Beatles or Christmas carols? What was it, Director Hayes?"

"Shut up, Joe," C. said.

Joe turned to me. "Promise me just one thing, Mack. Just one thing. If those crazies do end up killing me, which seems a lot likelier now than it did five seconds ago, promise me, if you survive me, that you will as governor get rid of this one-eared idiot. Promise me, Mack.

"Promise! My only wish! Do not deny a dying man his only wish!"

I just kept watching the fire burn up that Cessna 270 that I had just been riding in.

I was still thinking about the answer to Joe's earlier question about what all of this really was. Was it politics? Was it government?

What in the world was this I had gotten myself involved in?

At dinner that night Jackie and I talked about everything I did that day except my visit to Sandra Faye Parsons and the mummies. I was ashamed and disgusted with myself for what I wanted to do with Sandra Faye Parsons. Jackie was so smart that I was sure if I told her I had even been in that basement with Sandra Faye and the mummies, she would have figured out the rest.

And there I would have been, confessing and apologizing for what went on in my mind. It might have been all right for Jimmy Carter to admit in some dirty-magazine interview that he lusted in his heart for other women, but he wasn't married to Jackie.

Jackie and I ate Tex-Mex at the San Marcos Café on North-west Fiftieth, where everything was named after a city or town in Texas, which struck me as a dumb thing to do. But the food was the best Tex-Mex in Oklahoma City. I had the number-five combination, called The Austin City Limits, which was two

Lubbock cheese enchiladas, a Big Spring taco and a Denton tamale with Texarkana rice and Laredo beans. Jackie had The Kerrville Coach—three Wichita Falls beef tacos and a Beaumont burrito plus rice and beans. We both drank Amarillo iced tea and split a piece of Carthage pecan pie for dessert.

"Think what it must have been like for that poor man," she said of Tipp Freeman. "What would have happened to him if he had admitted it while he was still alive?"

"He would have been through politically, that is for sure," I said. "He would have probably had to move out of state. Some fool might even have tried to arrest him. I think it's against the law here to do . . . you know, what homosexuals do."

"What do they do, Mack?"

"I don't know and I do not want to know."

"How can there be a law against something that nobody knows what it is?"

"I did not make the law, Jackie."

"The novels never really spell it out either, do they? You know, describe exactly what homosexuals do."

No, Jackie dear, the novels I read, which were few and mostly about clean detectives, did not spell it out. I could not believe we were talking like this in a public restaurant over plates of Tex-Mex and Amarillo iced tea!

"Do you think that's the way it ought to be, Mack?" she said.

"It? What?"

"That homosexuals are treated the way they are, like criminals. There are a couple of men working for us I know are that way. They don't hurt anybody, they don't make passes at the truck drivers or warehousemen. Why should they be arrested? That's stupid."

"I am sure I agree with you."

"Then change things, Mack."

"I am the lieutenant governor, not God."

"You're my God and I think you should run for governor."

She had gotten to where she said something like this to me at least once a month. I always said, more or less, what I said now: "Not as long as Joe wants the job."

Joe, with all his problems, was the man who picked me to run with him the first time and time after time ever since. I would never turn on him no matter what he did. I just could not do that.

There was something Joe said about loyalty that I truly believed myself: "A politician who is disloyal deserves the worst—which is to be called a politician." Joe had a lot of sayings like that. A political science professor at OU had been talking about collecting them into a small book for the University of Oklahoma Press that he wanted to call *Buffaloisms— The Words and Wisdom of Governor Joe Hayman.* Joe thought the book and the title were both stupid and I pretty much agreed with him.

Jackie and I turned to the possible success of her son's plans for the post-oil society. I gave her my best eyewitness account of the Great Pouring at Oklahoma Blue Arrow.

She said: "You are such a better person than I am, Mack. I

could not have been there. I simply could not have done it. I am still so embarrassed about it and I hate myself for it. As one entrepreneur to another I admire him. I really do. But I really do feel my face warm up and my throat tighten up as a mother every time I have to tell somebody my son picks up old restaurant grease for a living. Will it ever pass, Mack?"

I told her I did not know.

And then we turned to the worst subject. The airplane explosion. She had been in a late-afternoon sales meeting when it happened and had heard only a few sketchy details from people in her office who had heard about it on the radio. That was fine with me. I told her what happened, but I left out enough of the details to make her believe my life had never really been at risk. It was a mistake. She pried it out of me anyhow and all it did was make it worse.

"So these madmen came within a few minutes of blowing you and that idiot Hayman to smithereens?" she said after a series of questions and answers and some sparring.

"You could say that, but we don't know for sure," I said.

Then I began to lay out some of the details of a new plan C., Buck and I were working on for apprehending the Ripper. This one would switch baits from Joe to me. I felt I had to tell her about it in case something did go wrong. She was my wife, after all. We did love each other, after all. She would sorely miss me, after all.

I was her God, after all.

She went Tulsa.

"No! I will not have it! You are the lieutenant governor! No!

Lieutenant governors do not do that kind of thing! No! Lieutenant governors are not bait for killers! No! I forbid it! No! Let them kill Joe! No! He deserves to die! No! Not you! No! I have already been a widow once! No! Not again! No!"

She never really calmed down. Not that night as she turned away from me in bed and sobbed, and not the next morning when I tried in vain to kiss her good-bye.

"I will wear the Chocolate Fork sash to your funeral, Mack! I promise you! I really will!"

That is what she yelled at me as I walked out the side door of our house to get into my blue Buick Skylark for the drive to the Big Boy at May and Reno.

■

C., Buck and I met for breakfast to work out the details of what we were to do next. We went to Big Boy because I flat refused to eat sitting three across in the backseat of C.'s command car. It was terrible and messy enough with two of us trying to have a meal back there. I was also still conscious of what Joe had said about how strange it was for grown men to eat their meals while riding around aimlessly through the streets of Oklahoma City.

No one had been killed or hurt in the airplane explosion and fire. But that was the extent of the good news from C. and Buck. Once firemen put it out and everything cooled off, the

FBI and OBI lab experts went to work on trying to figure out what had happened. They could find nothing conclusive. Nothing that would tie Jess or Jackson or any other person or persons known or unknown into the thing. The official best guess was that some exotic plastic explosive made in Czechoslovakia or some such place had been put into something electric that was triggered to go off at a certain time or when a certain thing happened on that airplane.

"A couple of minutes earlier could have made a huge hole in Joe's plans to become a mummy in the rotunda," said C., who was eating a short stack with bacon and coffee. I had a waffle with butter and warm maple syrup, plus grapefruit juice. Buck had some kind of granola or wheat-cereal thing with skim milk and fresh fruit.

I thought of saying, oh, yes, sir. It might also have interfered in a major way with some of my plans for future life as a nonmummy. But I said not a word. As time passed that morning I got closer and closer to being scared silent than I had ever been in my life.

The practical investigative scare, issue, dilemma, terror was that C. and Buck and all their people had no idea how Jess and/or Jackson had gotten anywhere near that Cessna. Neither of our villains had been out of sight or hearing since my Step One phone call to Jess that morning. Not for a second.

"So maybe they have somebody else working with them," Buck said.

"So maybe we must also think that maybe they're not it?" said C., as down and forlorn as I had ever seen him. The humor had suddenly drained out of him. "That there is somebody else or a group of somebody elses working this territory?"

"Working to kill Joe and me?"

"That seems so incredibly unlikely," Buck said.

I agreed and said so. Then, as if it were a perfectly natural thing to do next, I asked him if he could arrange for the FBI to give us a cut-rate price to check the fingerprints on twelve mummies that were now collecting dust, odors and embarrassing moments in an Enid, Oklahoma, basement.

"You are kidding me, I trust, suh," he said.

"I am not kidding," I said. "We are facing an identification task second to none. We are having trouble raising the money to do it. If the FBI could check fingerprints at cost—do you do things like that?"

"I don't know. I honestly don't know what our policy is on identifying mummies. I must say just off the top of my head that it would appear to be unlikely that our files would include the fingerprints of people like John Wilkes Booth. . . ."

"Gentlemen, if I may bring this back to our business at hand," C. said.

I acted like he hadn't said a thing and launched further into the full story of what I had seen and smelled in that basement in Enid. C. could not stand it for long.

"Shut up about those ___ mummies, Mack," he said. "I mean it. I really do not have the time to waste talking about mummies. I have got real dead people to talk about, to worry about. And so does Buck and so do you, Mister Lieutenant Governor."

So I said no more about mummies.

So we moved on to putting the final touches on the new plan. It was similar to the old one except for one major difference. I was the bait instead of Joe.

C. asked, "Maybe Jess and Jackson have absolutely nothing to do with any of this?"

"Well, suh," said Buck, "if that turns out to be so, and I am willing to bet the store it does not, then we have lost nothing except a little of the lieutenant governor's time and nerve endings."

Yes, suh.

■

The *Daily Oklahoman* had had three of our stories on its front page that morning. UNEXPLAINED EXPLOSION AND FIRE'S DE- STRUCTION OF STATE PLANE was the lead story. It was illus- trated with a three-column color photograph of firefighters attacking the blaze.

Then, on the left side, where what newspaper people call the off-lead, was the story of poor Willard (Tipp) Freeman: MUR- DERED LEGISLATOR WAS HOMOSEXUAL, PREACHER-COUSIN RE- VEALS. There was a one-column black-and-white photo of Freeman.

Then down in the left-hand corner was a much smaller story: BLUE ARROW PUTS OLD GREASE IN ITS BUS TANK. There with it was a two-column black-and-white picture of Governor Joe Hayman pouring the magic mixture into the gas tank of the GMC bus while Bill Hylton watched and smiled.

On the editorial page inside there was an editorial about the government of Oklahoma. Under the headline WHAT NEXT? one of the newspaper's hate-government editorial writers jumped Joe, C. and me for letting the wanton violence against us and others in the government continue unabated:

"Symbolically and satirically speaking, it could make Oklahomans wish more than just an airplane of the state government had been blown apart."

I found it to be a tasteless and irresponsible thing to say.

■

I heard the sound of a helicopter above when I stepped out of the Buick. And I saw cars and vans and people trying to look inconspicuous out of every corner of my one eye. If that Cessna hadn't blown up, I would probably have felt perfectly watched over, protected, safe, secure, invincible.

Instead, I was as scared as I had ever been in my life.

The receptionist just inside the door of Diamond Grove Hammers, Inc.'s Oklahoma City warehouse stood when I came in. She was a young black woman with her hair in tiny pigtails, like the lady who spoke the other day in Diamond Grove wore.

She said: "Welcome, Mr. Lieutenant Governor. Mr. Deaton

is expecting you. He said if he was not back in his office by the time you arrived, you should join him back in the warehouse. A new shipment of a new kind of hammer just arrived. The bottom part, the part that hits the nail, is square instead of round. And it's larger than your regular hammer. We're hoping it changes the faces of hammers everywhere. When there are new hammers to be made, Diamond Grove will make them. That's what Mr. Deaton says and he is right."

"I'm sure it will change the faces of hammers everywhere," I muttered. "I'm sure it will. Congratulations. On behalf of the governor and the legislature and the people of Oklahoma, congratulations. Hammers are the backbone and the future of our economy and our identity. Oklahoma, where the wind comes sweeping down the plain, will soon be as well known as Oklahoma, where the hammer comes banging down on the nail."

She looked at me with a twinkle of wonder and bewilderment in her two eyes.

All I was thinking about was: Expecting me? The woman said Jess was expecting me. How could he have been expecting me? This was supposed to be a surprise! The OBI/FBI team that had him under surveillance told us he had driven up from Diamond Grove early that morning.

Expecting me?

The young woman beckoned for me to follow her to a door to her right. It was the same one I went through the other day when I was here and Jess demonstrated the perfect hammer. When I was introduced to Jackson.

She opened the door. "I can find my way," I said.

"Fine. He should be back in the far right-hand corner," she said. "We're calling them the Big Jess."

"Calling what the Big Jess?"

"The new hammers with the square body."

"Oh, yes."

I walked in and she closed the door behind me. And suddenly I was absolutely terrified. I looked down at the microphone that was built into the top button of my suit coat. C. and Buck were three blocks away in a van waiting to listen to every word, to every sound.

Would they come when they heard the rat-tat-tat of machine-gun fire?

The place was lit bright by fluorescent lights. And there wasn't a sound. No music. Where was the music? Jess said he always listened to violins when he was in the warehouse.

I was certain somebody was watching me. Somebody with a machine gun of some kind. Or a cannon. Or a flamethrower.

Or a missile.

"Jess!" I yelled. "Jess! It's me, Mack!"

The only thing that happened was an echo. My own voice came back at me. Several times.

I took a few steps toward the right-hand corner of the warehouse. I entered one of the corridors made by boxes of hammers stacked head-high on both sides. There were ball-peen and small sledge hammers on the left, tack and copper-headed hammers on the right.

"Hey, Jess! I'm coming back where you are! Okay?"

I stopped to hear an answer.

There was none. And after my echoes got done, there was again absolute silence. Why wasn't the music on?

I wondered if Jackie was serious about wearing that stupid sash to my funeral. I wished that I, like Willard (Tipp) Freeman, had left behind some kind of instructions for my funeral. Don't cremate me, but don't lay me out like Johnny Whistle all made up like a girl. Keep the casket closed, please. Two songs, "Amazing Grace" and "Bringing in the Sheaves," both sung by huge church choirs. No lone soloists with accompanying piano players, no barbershop quartets, no guitar players or cowboy singers. No flowers, press or photographers inside the church. No graveside service. Just do it once in the church. And leave the rest to Brother Walt. Brother Walt was pastor emeritus of the First Church of the Holy Road in Adabel, Jackie's and my first hometown in Oklahoma. He was the best preacher and man in the whole world as well as our particular world. He loved us and we loved him, so much so that both of our twins, Tommy Walt and Walterene, were named for him. He had heart trouble and was up into his eighties now, but he could still outpreach, outsmart, outlove anybody. I could hear that deep eruption voice of his proclaiming the wonderfulness and goodness of his late departed friend, the One-eyed Mack. He would tell the story of my life, of how I came to him in Adabel a sinner and left a man of goodness and mercy. He would pour it on and on and on and he would make it sound right and true.

The imagined voice of Brother Walt was all I could hear at that moment.

I walked on. "Jess," I said more quietly. "Jess. I'm coming back to see you and the new Big Jess hammers. It's me, Mack. I understand they have square bottoms. Boy, when new hammers are made, Diamond Grove is sure going to make them. You can surely bet on that. We are so proud of you and Diamond Grove, Jess. On behalf of everyone in the Sooner State, let me say how proud we are of the company and the glory it has brought to Oklahoma. People all over the world have Diamond Grove hammers in their hands at this moment, I am sure. And with that hammer in their hand they are thinking of Oklahoma, the home of the best hammers in the world. Oklahoma, where the hammer comes down on the nail. Did you hear that, Jess? Oklahoma, where the hammer comes down on the nail."

I stopped talking. And this time I heard something. I took another step. And stopped. Like I was playing a game of Mother, May I.

"Jess?" I said.

Nothing.

So I started walking again. Five steps, ten steps. I heard something again. Was it a cough?

Again. Yes, a cough. Jess's cough!

"Jess, answer me. It's Mack. I'm coming your way."

I picked up the pace and suddenly I was in the right-hand corner of the warehouse.

There on the floor was Jess Deaton. He was lying on his back. Both of his arms were extended and there was a hammer lying by his right hand. It was a square-headed hammer, a Big

Jess, obviously. His skin was gray, almost like that of The Cluck on the couch, Johnny Whistle in the chair, Tip Freeman on the pavement. But Jess's eyes were open and he was breathing.

I went down to him.

"What happened, Jess?" I said.

"I'm going is what happened," he whispered. "I'm losing it."

"I'll call an ambulance," I said.

"Forget it. Put something under my head. I'll go out talking to you. Might as well be you as some paramedic."

There were several cellophane sacks of packing Styrofoam there on the floor. I grabbed one and slipped it under his head.

"Turn the music on," he said. His voice was weak, husky. "There's a switch over there on the wall."

I saw it. On the wall some ten feet away was something that resembled a huge light switch. "You sure it doesn't turn on any bombs or machine guns?" I said.

"You're safe," he said. "Be not a chicken."

"Why should I believe a mass murderer like you?"

"Turn the music on and shut up."

I walked over to the wall, thought of Jackie in her sash looking at my exploded remains before the casket was closed and threw the switch.

And from every corner of that warehouse came violin music.

"Isaac Stern playing Beethoven's Violin Concerto in D major," he said when I got back to him. "I want to go listening to him do that. Music to go to heaven by."

"You're not going anywhere near heaven, Jess. Killers of their fellow human beings do not go to heaven."

He started coughing. And I thought this was it, that wherever in the hereafter he was headed, the trip had just begun. The cough was so deep and awful and rattling that I was sure he would not survive. But he did. His eyes were open, his chest was still moving up and down. He was still alive.

"Where's Jackson?" I asked. I was down on my knees with my head not more than five inches from his. It was the only way I could hear.

A smile came to his face. "You want a truthful answer?"

"Yes."

"How much money do you need for those mummies?"

What? Well, now. I decided to go for the high bidder. "One hundred eleven thousand six hundred dollars."

"One-twenty-five will turn up in the account of that museum in Enid in a few days. I took care of it just a while ago."

"Hey, Jess. Thanks. Really, thank you."

"It's a bribe, Mack. My last bribe. You get the money, I get you to do something for me after I'm gone."

"What?"

"You'll see. It's honest and it's for the good."

"After you're dead, how will you know whether I do it or not?"

"You're an honest man."

Yes and no, I thought. No and yes. There are fine lines, I thought.

I said: "Okay. Go ahead and answer my question about Jackson."

Just like that, I said, Okay, go ahead. Okay, go ahead. Had I just accepted a bribe? My first bribe since coming into the service of the public as a county commissioner in Adabel more than twenty years before? If so, it was a most unusual bribe for a very good cause, but it was from a very bad man and I didn't even know what I was supposed to do in return.

Okay, go ahead.

"There were five Jacksons. All old subcontractors of mine. I made them all shave their heads and wear the same clothes so you fools would think there was only one of them."

"Where are they now?"

"Back in the woodwork where they came from."

"What do you mean, subcontractors?"

"That is none of your business."

He coughed again. Not quite as bad as before.

"You had a stupid plan," he said. "Coming in here like this to confront me. Trying to get me to kill Joe Hayman was even worse. I almost took you up on that one, though, just for the good of the people. An Oklahoma without Joe Hayman is a better Oklahoma. Your people are idiots."

"How did you know about our plan?"

"We've had you bugged every which way there is from the beginning."

"Bugged?"

"State-of-the-art stuff. Your FBI people probably don't know about it. Hayes and his idiots will never know about it.

I loved all that ___ and concealment they tried at the softball stadium. Your people are idiots."

I felt that another cough was coming on. I leaned away and looked around. Was there a sixth Jackson about to come around a corner any second with a hand-held missile launcher aimed at my stomach?

Jess did not cough. So I asked him: "Who are you, Jess? What were you? Subcontractors for what? Tell me that story."

"No."

"Why did you kill The Cluck and the others? Just because of Sooner Number One?"

"First, let me tell you that Doug Little was killed by his wife. We ran our own investigation. She apparently figured she could capitalize on the Capitol Ripper hysteria and take out her husband. She hired some mechanic, a guy who was screwing her, to fiddle with the steering. Tell C. and your idiot friends to pursue that and they shall find."

"Will do. Thanks. Sure . . ."

"Second, as best we can figure, Freeman jumped out of that window on his own. He, too, wanted it to appear to be murder, but it wasn't. The homosexual thing had him. If it had gotten out he would have been through. He needed the right wing, which is antihomosexual, so that was that. He was through so he ended it."

"How do you know that? How can you be so certain?"

"I know it, Mack. Shut up."

"All right, then, the other two. Johnny Whistle and The Cluck."

"I have nothing more to say," Jess said. His voice was much weaker now than when we started.

"Stick with us on Sooner Number One or die? Was that the message?"

"I have nothing more to say."

"How many others had you bought in the first place? How many did you have to send such a message to?" I could almost hear Buffalo Joe saying, "Now, that, Mack, is my idea of hardball politics. Stay bought or I'll kill you. Hardball politics, Mack. That is what that is."

But I could hear nothing from Jess. He clearly had almost no more time to say or do anything.

"You almost killed me and Joe last night," I said.

"That was triggered by remote control after you were out to make sure you weren't hurt. We were showboating a bit. We just wanted to scare you'all a bit."

"It worked."

He smiled. And that made him cough again. I moved my head away from his. The coughing got worse and worse. His whole insides seemed to be about to come right out of his mouth.

This time I was certain he would not be breathing when he was finished. And I was right.

I stayed there on my knees for several more seconds listening to the violin music of Isaac Stern before I realized I was really right, before I knew Jess Deaton was really dead.

A few seconds later I heard some commotion at the office end of the warehouse.

"Mack!" somebody yelled through a bullhorn over the music. It was C. "Deaton, this is Hayes! We're coming in!"

In a few seconds C., Buck and a battalion of men in suits and uniforms with pistols and rifles were all around me and the late Jess Deaton.

■

I believe in telling the truth and do so most of the time without having to think about it. But I also believe there are times when more good and less harm can be done with a lie than with the truth. Lying for the greater good, in the words of our governor. Right or wrong, in those last few seconds I made that decision about Jess's last few minutes.

"Everything was fine, coming in loud and clear, until the music started," C. said. "Then we lost everything but the violin."

Did Jess Deaton ask me to flip the music switch only so he could go to his maker listening to that Beethoven thing? Or was it also because he knew I was wired and he wanted to drown out our talk?

Dumb question.

"Did you get a death-bed confession, suh?" Buck asked.

The three of us had moved to another corner of the warehouse while the familiar army of technicians did their death-scene number on Jess.

"No," I said. "He died before we got to that."

"___!" C. said.

"All he said was that he was a contractor of some kind," I said.

Buck said, "One of my old sources said Deaton may have been a revolution contractor, a guy who toppled governments and leaders for a living. Not only for the United States of America but for anyone else who would pay his price. My old source was not sure and I could never run it down. But that would sure explain all of his money and why his records were clean."

C. turned on him. "Why didn't you tell us that?"

"Oh, calm down. I told you he did things for the government. The rest was speculation," Buck said. "What do we do now, Brother Hayes, is the only question of consequence for this moment."

C. looked at me for an answer.

"Why do anything?" I asked in my most innocent good-guy Mack tone.

"Well, it seems to me that what we probably have here is a death by natural causes," C. said. "And you could argue that that is all we have."

"Yes, suh," said Buck Sporne, the Pop Bottle Man's son.

"We can't prove any of the rest," C. said. "Until we can I suggest we keep it quiet."

"Yes, suh," said Buck. "It will remain forever our little secret."

Yes, suh.

I did not tell him one of Joe's favorite Buffaloisms about secrets:

"Keeping a secret, Mack, is like keeping a porcupine in a wet paper bag."

For two hours in Diamond Grove, Oklahoma, every school, every office, every restaurant and café, every store, even the service stations, were closed. All the cars and the delivery trucks stopped. Everything and everybody stopped because Jess Deaton was dead.

The memorial service was in the center of downtown. Those of us on the program were on the platform in front of city hall, where I had seen Jess present the dropout scholarships a few days earlier.

How many days ago was that anyhow? How much had happened since then?

People were crowded around the platform and up and down Main Street in front of the bank and the hotel and the department store and over and down the side streets in all directions. The police said more than twenty-five thousand people showed up, which was more than ten thousand more than the population of Diamond Grove. Those who could not see could at least hear on one of hundreds of public-address speakers set up throughout the town.

Everybody I saw was either crying or about to cry.

The mayor of Diamond Grove, a black man named Andrew H. Mackey, Jr., was the master of ceremonies. He worked as the assistant purchasing manager at the Diamond Grove Hammer plant and did the mayor's job on a part-time basis. That was how city government worked in most towns in Oklahoma.

"Don't think for one minute it's just the thousands of us here today," said Mayor Mackey. "Jess is here, all right. So is every God there is in heaven. Your God and my God and the God of the man and the woman and the kid and the stranger standing next to you this day in this place in this sunshine. We're all here. Everybody who matters is here. We matter. Every one of us matters. And we can prove it because of what Jess Deaton has done for us.

"And will do for us."

Mayor Mackey introduced a lawyer. His name was Eugene Tomkins.

"Jess Deaton left a will," said Eugene Tompkins, "and he left behind instructions that it be read aloud at this very spot on this very occasion—the occasion of his memorial service. 'At whatever kind of thing is put together,' was the way he put it.

"I will now read the will.

" 'I, Jess Deaton, being of sound mind, do hereby swear and attest that upon my death all of my earthly possessions be given to educating the people of Diamond Grove, Oklahoma.

The money will be managed, invested and dispersed by an elected committee of seven citizens.

" 'The committee shall have the absolute power to make all decisions on how the money is spent as long as none of it goes to any person, project or organization not located in or connected with the betterment of the city of Diamond Grove and its citizens. The lieutenant governor of Oklahoma, the One-eyed Mack, will be the eighth and only nonresident member of the committee. If he should die, resign or otherwise be unable to serve, no one will be designated to take his place.'

"And thus ends the reading of the will as prescribed by Jess Deaton and by the laws of the state of Oklahoma."

A terrific cheer came from the people down in front and it spread down the streets to the others. A chant got started.

"Jess! Jess! Hooray, Jess!

"Jess! Jess! Thank you, Jess!

"Jess! Jess! We love you, Jess!"

They had a lot to cheer about and to love Jess for. The newspapers had already reported that Deaton had left an estate valued at at least fifty million dollars, including the hammer company and the real estate in Diamond Grove. As C. had said, that was a lot of revolutions.

The newspapers, except for the *Oklahoman*, which still opposed it, were also predicting that Sooner Number One would pass overwhelmingly when it came to a vote in the legislature in a few weeks. Trying to raise Oklahoma's schools to a position higher than forty-five among the fifty states would now be done in the memory of Jess Deaton.

The newspapers had also run a story about how an anonymous donor had come forward to make it possible to unravel the mystery of the twelve mummies in the basement of the Museum of the Cherokee Strip in Enid. Sandra Faye Parsons was quoted as saying, "Within a year we may know which, if any, of these poor mummied souls, is, in fact, David E. George, alias John Wilkes Booth. That will be a great day for Oklahoma and Oklahomans."

Stephen Dobyns, the mystery writer-poet who was set to come to town anyhow that week, followed the lawyer by reading two of his poems. Neither of them rhymed and they were hard to follow, but I did like the second one, which was about what happens at death. The mind is tired so it gives up, but the body fights right to the end. He compared an aging body to a donkey being whipped by a man in a cart who is like the mind. It seemed to me that it should be the other way around, but, like I said, it was hard to follow. He was a friendly man with a terrific voice and he read his poetry beautifully. I had a high school English teacher in Kansas who said poetry was like music. Listen to it, she said, don't try to get it.

Seven people from Diamond Grove followed Dobyns to the microphone. Two of them were black, one of them Indian, one Hispanic. Each told a story about how his or her life had been changed by the generosity of Jess Deaton.

There was a young woman who had overcome drug addiction to go to law school and become an assistant United States attorney in Tulsa. There was a young man who had come out of prison after serving a term for armed robbery. A program funded by Jess helped him to earn his high school diploma and then a junior college degree. He now owned and operated one of those quick lubrication places, which did for cars what Jack-ieMarts did for people in need of groceries and other basics. Another man now played first-chair viola in the Houston Symphony Orchestra because of Jess's insistence that every student at Diamond Grove High School learn how to play a musical instrument. Jess paid for all the instruments.

The most moving story was told by a young Choctaw man in a wheelchair. He had been a junior at the OU medical school when a tractor-trailer plowed into his little Toyota during a thunderstorm on I-35 near Tonkawa.

"I lost both of my legs and any hope of finishing medical school and my dream of becoming the leading family doctor back home here in Diamond Grove," the man told the crowd. "It was so bad, in fact, that I thought seriously about simply taking my own life. What was the point of going on?

"Well, then Jess Deaton came to see me. I was back home but just barely. He told me that if I had the guts and the gumption and the desire to go on, that he would kick me in the butt and he would pay for it. He got several prominent people around the country who had overcome bigger physical handicaps than mine to call me on the phone. He hired a psychiatrist from the Menninger Foundation in Topeka, Kansas, to drop in on me unexpectedly to offer counsel and guidance—and therapy.

"Jess Deaton bought me some hope and gave it to me. He

saved my life. As many of you know, I am, in fact, a physician in Diamond Grove. I see out there now the faces of many of my patients, my people.

"I owe everything to . . ."

The man was crying. He could not finish his sentence.

I was the last speaker. Joe had decided it was not appropriate for a governor to speak at the funeral of a man we knew but could not prove was responsible for the murder of a few members of the Oklahoma legislature and the destruction of a state-owned Cessna 270. It was all still a secret, of course, but Joe said it would eventually get out. Everything eventually gets out. And how would we explain then what he was doing at that crazy killer's funeral? But what if it didn't get out? I argued. How could you explain not going to the funeral of one of Oklahoma's most prominent citizens who had done so much for education and culture in his city and our state?

We worked it out by agreeing that Joe would be called out to western Oklahoma on another personal emergency and I would attend the memorial service and represent the governor and all of state government.

Joe, in jest, had suggested I do for Jess what the cousin-preacher had done for Tipp Freeman. "Say something like, By the way, Jess wanted me to announce here today that he was a cold-blooded mass murderer. He, in fact, did away with at least two members of the Oklahoma legislature and who knows how many other people in the course of a long and distinguished career that preceded his return to Oklahoma. He also blew up a Cessna airplane owned by the state of Oklahoma, paid for with 1.2 million dollars of your tax money."

I had no intention of saying anything like that.

I began: "Jess Deaton, unlike many other people of wealth, left a legacy of spirit in addition to that of buildings and things. This town, this state, will never be the same because of him. He made us all see what money, spent wisely, can do. He put to rest once and for all the old saw that throwing money at something is no solution. He proved that there are some things that throwing money at will help. Like educating people about their culture as well as the regular things we call reading, writing, arithmetic, history, science and all the rest. The next time you read about some millionaire flying off to Rio or Europe with seven hundred of his closest friends for a birthday party or buying the Dallas Cowboys or five racehorses or six Rolls-Royces or a yacht that sleeps fifty, remember Jess Deaton.

"Remember Jess Deaton because he made a difference. He came back to Diamond Grove with his suitcase full of money to make a difference. He came back here because he knew his suitcase would make a difference here. He set an example for everybody with suitcases full of money from this day forward to follow.

"Hey, you out there, you people with suitcases full of money! Look what Jess Deaton did with his! Look what you could do with yours!

"Hey, you out there, remember Jess Deaton!"

Somebody started a chant.

"Jess! Jess! Remember Jess!

"Jess! Jess! We love you, Jess!

"Jess! Jess! You were the best!

"Jess! Jess! Good-bye, Jess!"

I thought the cheering and the tears would never stop, not even long enough for me to finish what I had come to say. All I had left that I had come prepared to say were some final thank-yous and good-lucks.

But then, as I listened to the cheers and watched the tears flow from the eyes of all those people, I knew I had to say something else. I could not let it end this way. I could not cut the line this fine.

I could live with having lusted after Sandra Faye Parsons. I could even live with having accepted the mummy bribe from Jess. But I could not live with this, not this. Not me, a mostly good and honest man. Not now, not ever.

So, after the people got quiet again, I said what I had not come to say.

I said:

"I wish that was all I had to say this day about Jess Deaton. I wish that all that needed to be said had been said. But there is more, ladies and gentlemen, boys and girls of Diamond Grove. There was more to Jess Deaton, another side to Jess Deaton, as there is to all of you and to me and to everyone else in this world. We are none all good or all bad. We are all always walking along on either side of a fine line. Sometimes we are on that side, sometimes on the other. But all of us are walking. All of us."

One of the reasons my speech to the Democrats at Madison Square Garden went over in such a large way with David Brinkley and everyone else was the fact that I was a good public speaker. That's not bragging, really it isn't; that is a simple fact. I knew how to raise and lower the pitch and the volume, change the tone and the mood. I knew how to gesture, to pause and do all the other things a speaker should do to capture and hold an audience. Videotapes of my New York speech were used in high school speech classes in at least three high schools in Oklahoma—those in Kingfisher, Seminole and Tishomingo. Pardon the boasting, but how many people, even lieutenant governors, can claim that kind of special attention?

The audience now out there on the streets and the sidewalks and the yards of Diamond Grove was absolutely silent. They were listening to me like they had probably never listened to anything else like this before in their lives.

I had never said or done anything like this before in my life.

"It is with deep sadness and regret, my friends of Diamond Grove, that I must tell you that in addition to being a savior of people and spirits, he was also a killer of people and spirits."

"No!" somebody yelled.

"Shut up, Mack!" somebody else yelled.

"Sit down, Mack."

"Go back to Oklahoma City, where you belong!"

But the shouters were soon silenced by the silence of the others.

Go on, Mack, they said. Go on. Whatever it is, tell us. We're listening.

"It might not have been provable in a court of law, but top law-enforcement people in the state and federal government believe your beloved Jess was behind the killing of at least two of the state legislators who passed from us to their reward last week. We believe he drove a third to take his own life."

There were some quiet squeals and screams and murmurs and *no*'s from the audience.

"Good riddance!" somebody yelled.

"Who cares?" somebody else screamed.

But soon all was quiet again for me to proceed.

"We should all care. How can we not care? How can we not care that Jess Deaton was a murderer? He committed his murders—or had them committed, we believe—because he cared so deeply about the Sooner Number One legislative proposal. He very much wanted it to succeed, to become law so that others in Oklahoma could reap some of the same kind of rewards you in Diamond Grove had from his leadership, vision and resources. He saw those legislators as barriers to that and he acted.

"He cannot be forgiven for that. No matter his reasons, murder cannot be condoned nor can it be ignored by me or you or anyone else. Jess Deaton was a generous, caring and visionary man. He was also an evil and destructive man. We must know that, accept it and move on to a realistic memory of Jess Deaton."

I took a deep breath and stole a glance around at Mayor

Mackey. His eyes were closed, his face was twisted and turned like it had been hit by a truck. A Mack truck. The man was in agony. But he was listening.

Everyone was listening.

I went on: "It is difficult to understand how the capacity to save the life of the young doctor who spoke a few moments ago and to take the life of a young legislator as he did a few days ago can be contained in the mind and soul of the same person. But Jess Deaton had that capacity. He lived on the outer limits of both evil and good at the same time.

"Maybe there is at least a little of that in all of us. Could that be true? Could it be that maybe there was simply more of both extremes in Jess than normal?"

Somebody started the chant again.

"Jess! Jess! Remember Jess!"

It was not picked up by many people this time and soon it was quiet again.

I said: "Yes, yes, remember Jess. None of us should ever forget Jess Deaton. None of us should ever forget the good side of Jess Deaton, the side most of us saw and appreciated—and benefitted from."

"Yes! Yes! Remember Jess!

"Yes! Yes! Remember Jess!

"Yes! Yes! Remember Jess!"

And when it was quiet again, I said:

"I certainly benefitted. Shortly before he died I asked him to help me and the state historical society finance a special project for which regular state funds were not available. He granted my wish in exchange for doing what I am about to do now.

"Which is to say to one and to all, I hereby accept the appointment to serve on the commission that will decide how his legacy to you, the residents of Diamond Grove, will be managed and distributed.

"If that constitutes a bribe, then so be it. I hereby confess and beg for mercy."

The people of Diamond Grove erupted again with cheers and chants and applause.

I had nothing more to say. I had just finished the best and most important speech of my life. The mummy speech to the Democratic convention was now and forever in second place.

I sat down and Mayor Mackey got up and went to the microphone.

"Well, all right now. What an awful thing we have just heard about our man Jess. What would be even more awful would be if we didn't know it. The lieutenant governor did us a tough and good deed just now. He really did. We had to know. We just had to know this about Jess."

His face went back to looking like it had been smashed by a Mack. Only this time it was wet from large tears. He sat down again.

It was left to Isaac Stern to end it.

Mr. Stern had flown in with Dobyns on a Tulsa oilman's private jet that morning from New York City. He was a short, fat, delightful man who laughed and smiled and kidded around like real people do. More, actually, than many of the real people I knew, in fact. I liked him so much, I wanted to ask Isaac Stern to stay and live with us in Oklahoma. But that would have been a stupid thing for me to say and impossible for him to do.

He stepped to the microphone with his violin and bow. He told the crowd he remembered with happiness his day in Diamond Grove the previous year.

"I am here today for the same reason all of you are," he said. "We have just heard that there was another side to this man. So be it. I am here to honor the special side that knew the real value of money."

There was a brief cheer, and then Stern took a handkerchief from his suit coat pocket, put it on top of his violin and stuck it under his chin.

He brought his bow to the violin, nodded to the leader of the Strings of Diamond Grove and away they went. The sound was that of Beethoven's Ninth Violin Concerto.

After a few minutes a small single-engine airplane appeared overhead, flying very low from the south. Everybody on the platform and even down on the lawn and the streets knew it would be coming and why.

The plane dipped its left wing toward the ground and then made two large circles over the town.

We knew what was happening. In accordance with his wishes, Jess's body, like Tipp Freeman's, had been cremated and the ashes were being sprinkled down on the people of Diamond Grove.

The plane then flew away and disappeared again to the south.

The music continued, filling the town for another twenty minutes or so.

And everyone there probably forever.

About the Author

This is JIM LEHRER's eighth novel—the
sixth about the One-eyed Mack. He is
also the author of two books of nonfiction
and three plays and he co-anchors the
MacNeil/Lehrer NewsHour on PBS. He
and his wife, Kate, live in Washington,
D.C. They have three daughters.